Deadly Trail

Ace Brabbin, a Confederate secret agent during the war, is recruited by his former boss, to prevent the assassination of a territorial governor. The threat to the governor springs from his intention to introduce unpopular and controversial equality legislation for Blacks and Indians. He will reveal his plans in a speech in a town called Cheyney.

Knowing that the assassin will be on the stage travelling to Cheyney, Brabbin goes undercover to unmask him. But like all good plans, it backfires. Apache renegades attack the stage, forcing it to divert to the ghost town of Banyon where the travellers are left stranded.

Will the assassin receive his comeuppance? Will the governor be safe and will Brabbin escape with his life? These and many other questions will only be answered when this exciting tale draws to its dramatic close.

Deadly Trail

JACK HOLT

A Black Horse Western

ROBERT HALE · LONDON

00253202

ISBN 0 7090 7079 9

Robert Hale Limited
Clerkenwell House
Clerkenwell Green
London EC1R 0HT

Typeset by
Derek Doyle & Associates, Liverpool.
Printed and bound in Great Britain by
Antony Rowe Limited, Wiltshire.

ONE

'Hold it right there, mister!'

Ace Brabbin froze on the steps of the Cat's Tail saloon, shoulders tensing. Two oldsters lolling on the saloon porch slid out of their chairs and hurried away. One of the men tipped his hat and greeted:

'Howdy, Sheriff.'

'Morning, Tod,' the voice behind Brabbin answered. It was a voice with a no-nonsense tone to it.

'Rufus,' he greeted the second man.

The old-timers ate up yards to get out of the range of gunfire should that happen, and it looked likely. They joined the gathering of curious citizens already forming in the wings.

Bell Creek was a quiet, law-abiding town – a family town. That it was so, was down to the lawman who had challenged Brabbin.

'I'm Sheriff Luther Spencer,' he identified himself. 'Don't turn. Drop your gunbelt.'

'Is this the way you greet all your visitors?' Brabbin asked calmly. 'I haven't been in town long enough to have done any wrong. I've just hitched my horse, Sheriff.'

'Too long for your kind. Got a dodger with your dial on it, and a wire telling me to arrest you for murder. I'm to hand you over to a US marshal at Cheyney, if you showed. You've shown,' he stated grimly.

'What if I don't want to be handed over to this US marshal, Sheriff?' Brabbin asked icily.

'You'll be handed over,' Spencer stated bluntly. 'Standing or boxed. All the same to me, Brabbin. I guess that makes the next move yours.'

Brabbin turned slowly – steely grey eyes locking with the sheriff's.

'I told you not to turn,' Spencer grated, his hand hovering over his .45.

Ace Brabbin grinned. 'Guess I never was much good at obeying orders, Sheriff. Besides,' Brabbin's voice dropped a notch, 'I like to face the man who challenges me, before I . . .' He let the implied threat hang in the air.

Luther Spencer did not budge. His stance remained rock steady. The gambler admired the lawman's grit.

'Are you planning on making a play, Brabbin?'

'Maybe,' the gambler said. 'I'm thinking that I might not have a choice, if you persist in bucking me, Sheriff.'

'You're wanted for murder,' There was not a shred of compromise in the lawman's tone. 'That means I've got to take you in.' Spencer sighed wearily. '1 wish you'd given my town a wide berth. But you haven't. So . . .'

'I'm no slouch with an iron,' Brabbin warned the sheriff. 'What if I tell you the gent back in Traders Crossing challenged me, and I acted in self-defence?'

'You can say anything you please, mister. It isn't up to me to believe or disbelieve what you say. A jury will do that.'

Ace Brabbin chuckled. 'A jury, huh. What do you figure my chances are, Sheriff? I'm a gambler. Folk don't like gamblers much.'

'No one forced you to be a gambler, Brabbin,' Spencer said unsympathetically.

'Sometimes circumstances dictate a man's path, Sheriff. And there isn't a whole lot a man can do about it.'

'We can talk 'round this all day, Brabbin,' Spencer growled. 'And at the end I'll still have to take you in and hand you over. So let's settle it one way or 'nother.' Spencer's stance changed. 'I'll ask you again to shuck your iron.'

Ace Brabbin heaved in a long breath. 'Don't think I'm of a mind to do that, Sheriff.'

'Don't go for it, gambler,' the lawman advised.

Brabbin said: 'Figure I could take you?'

Spencer said drily: 'Figure you won't get the

chance.' He glanced beyond the gambler to the saloon. 'Ned. Get out here.'

The saloon bat-wings parted. Spencer's deputy stepped through, toting a shotgun.

'Move and you're dead!' he cautioned Brabbin.

Ace Brabbin stiffened. 'Sneaky, Sheriff.'

'But effective,' the lawman replied. 'That's a Greener my deputy is packing. Twitch and he'll blow you all the way to Mexico.'

The gambler let the seconds tick by, each one getting quieter as the hush gripping the town deepened.

'Ned's impatient, too,' Spencer cautioned. 'It's a real risk to make an impatient man toting a shotgun edgy.'

By now the street was crowded. Bets were being placed on the outcome of the impasse between the gambler and the law. Anyone willing to put their money on Brabbin were getting long odds on him coming out of the confrontation standing. Some were of the opinion that Brabbin's thonged, low-slung Colt .45 would clear leather lightning fast, and they placed their bets accordingly.

'If he draws another breath,' Ed Benteen, the general store owner opined, 'Ned will make him a harp player.'

'You figure?' a carrot-haired man standing alongside Ed Benteen quizzed. 'The gambler looks fast.'

8

'Fast is no darn good when buckshot is coming your way,' another man said.

'I agree with, Ed,' the roly-poly town medic said. 'The gambler doesn't stand a chance in Hades! Ned Belton will spread him all over Main.'

The tension had built up relentlessly since Spencer had put in his challenge, until now a bird's call in an oak near the saloon sounded as loud as thunder in the tomblike stillness.

'This shotgun is getting real heavy,' Ned Belton warned. 'Soon I'll have to use it or drop it, gambler.'

'Don't shoot yourself in the foot, Deputy,' Brabbin said calmly.

Ed Benteen said: 'Shucks. That card-sharp's got nerve!'

'Sounds like you're on that gambler's side, Ed,' the livery owner accused.

Benteen said: 'Well, you got to admire a man with guts, Spike.'

'Guts, huh?' Spike snorted. He cut loose with a long stream of tobacco juice that vanished the instant it hit the dust of the street. 'Dumb, I'd say.'

The stand-off was momentarily interrupted by the arrival of the stage thundering along Main to come to a wheel-locking stop outside the Fargo depot, churning up a cloud of swirling dust. Heads were already craning out of the window to take in the stand-off outside the Cat's Tail. The stage passengers quickly formed a huddled group

9

outside the Fargo depot to watch the unfolding drama.

'Seems like we should have sold tickets, Sheriff,' Ace Brabbin drawled. 'Looks like we'd have made quite a penny.'

'No pockets on a shroud,' Spencer observed, in a tone as dry as Mojave sand.

Brabbin glanced up at the lordly gent who had put in an appearance on the hotel veranda. He nodded to the hotel directly behind the sheriff. 'Looks like we're getting a better type of spectator, Sheriff.'

Spencer grinned. 'I'll have to take your word for that.'

Brabbin laughed. 'You don't trust me, Sheriff?'

'As much as I'd trust a rattler,' the lawman returned bluntly.

'Let's get this over with, Luther,' his deputy griped.

'Getting a touch nervous, Deputy?' Ace Brabbin taunted Belton.

'I ain't nervous,' the deputy roared back. 'I've dealt with a thousand maggots like you, Brabbin. Prob'ly deal with a thousand more, too.'

'If you're still sucking air,' Brabbin replied in a dead tone.

Goaded, the deputy lunged at Brabbin, shot-gun-butt raised to inflict bone-crushing injury. Spencer knew that the gambler's chewing on Belton's nerves had worked. He had lifted the threat of the shotgun. It was butt forward, and useless.

With the speed of a lizard's tongue, Brabbin ducked. Belton tumbled forward. The gambler stepped behind him. Belton, legs and hands flailing, crashed down the saloon steps. The sheriff danced to one side, but was unsighted for a couple of vital seconds.

The Greener clattered to the ground and exploded, scattering the crowd. Ace Brabbin now had the upper hand. A pistol cracked. A bullet tore a chunk of wood from the porch at the gambler's feet.

Brabbin's hand stalled over his Colt .45.

'The next one will be right between your eyes,' the man on the hotel veranda warned Brabbin, in a Georgian accent. 'Your prisoner I believe, Sheriff.'

Scowling at his deputy, the lawman picked up the discharged shotgun. Luckily no one had been maimed or killed. He took two shells from his vest pocket, broke the gun and slotted them in. Then he pointed the shotgun at Brabbin and ordered:

'Shuck the iron. Now!'

The gambler pitched his gun to the sheriff's feet.

'Pick it up, Ned,' Spencer growled. 'And try not to shoot yourself.'

Sullen-faced, Belton grabbed the gun. He would have gladly used it on Brabbin.

'Start walking, Brabbin.' Spencer nodded to the south end of Main. 'The jail is that way.' He turned to the man on the hotel veranda. 'Obliged, mister.'

'My pleasure, Sheriff,' the expensively dressed man answered smoothly.

The cell door clanged shut on Ace Brabbin. 'What now, Sheriff?'

'An hour and we board the stage for Cheyney.'

'Rough terrain. Indians – Apache renegades. Worst kind.'

'Blood Wing and his ragtag bunch have been acting up some.'

Ace Brabbin lounged on his bunk, his hands behind his head. 'How far is Cheyney, Sheriff?'

'Thirty miles, give or take.'

'A long way.' Brabbin yawned and closed his eyes. 'Yes, sir. A long way.'

Spencer snorted. 'Not long enough when there's a noose waiting.'

'Might never get to wear that noose, Sheriff,' the gambler speculated.

'I aim to see that you do,' the Bell Creek lawman stated.

'Guess we'll have to wait and see about that,' Brabbin said.

'We should hang the bastard here and now,' was Ned Belton's opinion.

The gambler chuckled. 'Why, Deputy, you'd probably go and hang yourself by mistake.'

Belton was diving for Brabbin, murder in mind. Spencer blocked his path and manhandled him back to the law-office.

'Look, Brabbin,' the sheriff said, 'we've only got an hour to wait for the stage's departure. But that's long enough for Ned to send you to Hades. So my advice is to sit and shut.'

Spencer stormed through the connecting door to the law-office, slamming it behind him. A couple of minutes later a hand came to the cell window and slipped an envelope to Brabbin. He quickly read its contents. He then shredded the sheets of paper. He went to the window and let them blow away on the breeze.

TWO

'All 'board!'

The Fargo driver's yell reached into every corner of Bell Creek, bringing the passengers for the stage from the hotel, saloon, and jail. The red-haired Kate Branigan came from the office of the *Bell Creek Sentinel*. She held a stub of pencil, scribbling in the last details of her current story for the newspaper, almost colliding with Ace Brabbin as he boarded the stage. The reporter's vanity case slipped from her grasp. The lock sprang open. She quickly retrieved the case and relocked it.

'Ma'am,' the gambler said, 'I'd help, but. . .' He turned to show his hands bound behind his back with a rawhide ligature.

'Step aside,' Spencer snapped. 'Sorry about that, Kate.'

'No harm done, Luther,' she replied, flashing a mischievous emerald-green eye Ace Brabbin's way.

'You're the *Bell Creek Sentinel*'s lead story tomorrow, Mr Brabbin.' She handed over her scribbled copy to the boy running alongside her. 'I've just finished writing it.'

The gambler's smile was as charming as he could make it, which was considerable.

'Then I'm sure it will be a very good story.' He grinned wickedly. 'Kate.'

Sheriff Spencer glowered. Not at Brabbin's brazenness, but at Kate Branigan's welcoming response.

'Wipe that sneer off your dial, mister!' the Bell Creek lawman ordered his prisoner.

Quick-eyed as a polecat, Brabbin had noticed the derringer Kate had tucked away in her vanity-case. Interesting, he thought.

'That person cannot surely be travelling on this stage,' Prudence Johnson, the president of Bell Creek's Committee for Clean Living and Racial Purity huffed, sniffing the air with a cherry-tipped nose, due to a chill she had caught while trying to barricade the entrance to the Cat's Tail saloon the previous night. 'Driver,' she summoned.

Andy Wright leaned off the box. 'Miss Johnson, ma'am?'

'I refuse to travel on the same stage as this . . . this,' her face curled in distaste, 'person.'

'Got a ticket for the card wizard, Sheriff?' Wright asked Spencer.

'He's paid for as far as Cheyney, Andy.'

Wright shrugged. 'I guess he's got a right, Miss Johnson.'

Prudence Johnson scowled. 'Really!'

'Cheyney ain't far, Prudence,' Sheriff Spencer said. 'Mightn't even be that far, if the US marshal coming for Brabbin continues along the trail.'

Unmoved by Spencer's arguments, Prudence Johnson declared, 'Thirty miles is much too long to be in this killer's company, Sheriff Spencer. I shall not vote for you come the Fall election.'

She had not voted for him last time either. But Spencer thought it wise not to tell her so.

'Inside,' he ordered Ace Brabbin.

The only seat left was between Prudence Johnson and Kate Branigan, which the sheriff occupied, much to Prudence Johnson's relief and Kate Branigan's amusement.

'Sit on the floor,' Spencer told the gambler.

'I'm sure if we squeeze up, Mr Brabbin will—'

'Certainly not!' Prudence Johnson declared, in an admonishing tone.

Brabbin said: 'Thank you, Kate. I can see that you're of a kindly and Christian nature.'

It was, Brabbin reckoned, as he suspected. Kate Branigan had offered her invitation more to tease Prudence Johnson than out of any concern for his comfort. Evidence of her mischief was there in her emerald-green eyes. Ace Brabbin's glance told her that she was not fooling him. It did not seem to

16

bother her. Kate Branigan, he decided, was a mighty cool-headed and finely proportioned woman.

'How does it feel to be a killer, Mr Brabbin?' Kate enquired.

Brabbin's gaze held hers, unflinching. 'Are you asking as a woman or as a newspaper reporter, Kate?'

'Both, I guess,' was her reply.

'How could this man possibly interest you, Miss Branigan?' asked Prudence Johnson. 'No lady should even talk to such a man.'

'You're entitled to your opinion, Miss Johnson,' said Kate starchily. 'And I'm entitled to pick the men I talk to.'

Prudence Johnson drew herself upright in her seat, her eyes aflame with indignation.

'Well?' Kate asked Brabbin. 'What's it like to be a killer?'

'I wouldn't know. I'm not a killer, Kate,' Brabbin answered.

'Word has it that you shot a man in cold blood,' the reporter said. 'What else can you be but a killer, Mr Brabbin?'

'The lady's got a point!' This was the opinion of a heavy-shouldered man called Amos Stradden, a rancher.

'I'd say I defended myself against a damn tinhorn,' Brabbin flung back.

'I'll remind you, sir, that there's a lady of delicate constitution on board this stage.' Stradden's eyes were firmly fixed on Prudence Johnson as the lady whose welfare concerned him.

The reports on the stage passengers which had been slipped through his cell window had informed Brabbin that Amos Stradden was Bell Creek's wealthiest citizen, but noted that his wealth was something of a mystery. He had a fine ranch, but it was not big enough to fill his coffers to the extent that they bulged.

'Pardon, ma'am,' Brabbin apologized to Prudence Johnson. 'Mr Stradden is right. There's no call for swearing.'

Miss Johnson settled herself smugly into the seat, dismissive of the gambler's apology.

'Thank you for coming to my aid, Mr Stradden, sir,' she said.

The rancher tipped his hat. 'My pleasure, ma'am.'

An old woman who sat in the corner alongside Stradden, Miss Gertrude Bletchley, whom Ace Brabbin had had a sense of familiarity with on first seeing her, but had dismissed the notion because she had the kind of round grandmother's face that seemed familiar to everyone on sight, complimented the rancher on his defence of Prudence Johnson's and her sensibilities.

'Seems you're a bad lot, Mr Brabbin,' said Kate Branigan.

The gambler grinned. 'Seems so, Kate.'

Prudence Johnson sniffed the air, and scowled at the reporter for continuing her familiarity with Brabbin, when it was clearly the wish of her fellow-travellers that he be ostracized.

A silence fell. The only interruption was the rattle and creak of the stage as it made swift progress over the trail whose state of repair had taken a turn for the worse during a recent storm, making the stage sway and bounce, sometimes alarmingly so.

Kate Branigan broke the silence.

'Folks reckon that you're a fast draw, Mr Brabbin.'

'I'd be pleased if you called me Ace, Kate?'

She laughed, and to Brabbin's ears it sounded like a dozen heavenly harps had just been played.

'So, how fast are you?'

'Lightning fast, as I hear it,' came Luther Spencer's reply.

'Does that answer your question, Kate?' Brabbin drawled lazily.

'I guess it does at that . . . Ace.'

'Really!' Prudence Johnson exploded. Her black-marble eyes bored with a fiery disapproval into Kate Branigan's.

'So why did you draw on this Dandon fella?' Kate asked.

Ace Brabbin got the notion that the reporter's curiosity about his motivation sprang from a personal rather than a professional interest in him. Being a red-blooded male, it pleased him to think so.

'He called me a cheat.'

Kate Branigan arched an amused eyebrow. 'You're a gambler. I would have thought that being called a cheat is an occupational hazard.'

Brabbin agreed.

'Do you always kill your accusers?' The question came surprisingly from Gertrude Bletchley, whom everyone thought had dozed off.

'No, ma'am. I try not to.'

'Hah!' Prudence Johnson snorted.

'Damn gamblers!' Amos Stradden swore.

'Why, sir,' Brabbin intoned with just the right amount of righteousness, 'remember, there are ladies present.'

Riled at having the tables turned on him, the beefy rancher started forward in his seat, fists balled. 'Why you—'

Sheriff Spencer shoved Stradden back into his seat. 'The haul to Cheyney isn't a long one. But it could be a mighty troublesome one if we all start going off half-cocked. You button your lip, Brabbin,' the lawman ordered. 'And show respect.'

'Afraid Stradden won't vote for you either, Sheriff?'

Now it was Spencer's turn to start forward in his seat.

'Is that smoke?' Kate Branigan's question shunted all other considerations aside.

'Apaches, you reckon?' a small-framed man with wispy fair hair called Walter Hanley fretted.

News of Apache atrocities had been filtering through to Bell Creek over the previous couple of days. A band of angry bucks, fed up with life on the reservation, had absconded to join up with Blood Wing, a renegade chief who had fled to Mexico rather than embrace the demeaning life the whiteman planned for them. They were a sizable group of about fifty braves, and had begun raiding and pillaging at random.

'Raids with no pattern that the army can get a handle on,' a prospector sheltering in Bell Creek had told the patrons of the Cat's Tail saloon a couple of nights previously. 'Slaughtered a farmer and his family a coupla days back, just for the hell of it. Then rode like the wind to do the same forty miles away to the east the next day, takin' every scalp for the takin'. Takin' the women too.'

The prospector's hair-raising stories now came racing back to the stagecoach passengers. Heads craned out of the stage windows to look at the rising smoke. Everyone had an opinion.

'Not Indian smoke,' Ace Brabbin said.

'You an expert?' Hanley asked spikily – his pale face that saw little of the outdoors flushing with colour. He clutched the satchel he was carrying even closer to his chest than it had been since the start of the journey, as if it held his eternal soul.

'Woodsmoke,' said Brabbin. 'Burning brush, I reckon.'

An air of relief swept the passengers; a relief that was short lived when Brabbin said: 'Not woodsmoke.' They followed his glance to the left and rear of the stage where puffing clouds rose from a ridge. 'Apache smoke,' he confirmed.

Stradden was most affected by the news.

'Apaches?'

The nervous twitch on the rancher's cheek was not missed by Brabbin. The colour drained from Stradden's sun-coppered face.

'Are you sure?' the rancher challenged Brabbin.

'I'm sure.'

'You can read the smoke, Brabbin?' Spencer asked.

'Yes.'

'What does it say?'

'Just let's say that they know we're around, Sheriff.'

'And . . . ?' the lawman prodded.

Brabbin glanced to the rising smoke. 'Seems they have a couple of wagons in their sights, too.'

'Wagons, you say?' The sharply asked question was Gertrude Bletchley's.

'Yes, ma'am,' the gambler said. 'I guess if this *hombre* Blood Wing is only after scalps and women, our safety will depend on how many scalps there are in those wagons. How many women for the bucks to enjoy. And how well armed Blood Wing reckons they are.'

Prudence Johnson's hand shot to her mouth and she swayed in the seat. Tut-tutting, Miss Bletchley consoled her:

'We must be half-way to Cheyney by now. So I figure that we'll there before this Blood Wing can catch us up, dear.'

'Don't reckon so, ma'am,' said Luther Spencer, spotting a half-dozen braves on a ridge to the south of the trail within easy striking distance, if they were of a mind to attack the stage.

Amos Stradden, his fear under control, proclaimed with a steely resolve, 'Let them try and we'll send them to hell.'

'Hadn't you better give Ace a gun, Sheriff?' Kate Branigan asked.

'A gun?' Spencer yelped. 'To give him the chance to shoot us all? I reckon that would be a mite unwise, Miss Branigan, ma'am.'

'You can't leave him defenceless,' she argued. 'Besides, it looks like we'll need all the firepower we can muster.'

Prudence Johnson gave the sheriff her backing. 'The sheriff is right. Give that killer a gun and what's to stop him—'

'Fiddley!' All eyes turned to Gertrude Bletchley. 'Like Miss Branigan said, we'll likely need his gun before this journey is much older.'

'No gun for Brabbin!' Luther Spencer uncompromisingly announced. 'He stays hog-tied 'til I hand him over to the US marshal. 'That's an end of it,' he growled, as Kate was about to protest further.

'A sensible decision, Sheriff Spencer,' Prudence Johnson complimented.

The wispy-haired Walter Hanley added his endorsement to Johnson's. Amos Stradden did not offer an opinion either way. But Ace Brabbin reckoned that if he had, it would be for Spencer giving him a gun. Not because he felt any moral indignation at leaving a man defenceless in the face of danger, or that he would turn the gun on his fellow-passengers, but because of the fear that had been stalking him since the second that the Indians had expressed an interest in them. Fear of the Apache was not uncommon. In fact any man who was not afraid could safely be termed loco.

'Why are those heathen savages just sitting there watching us like vultures?' The question was Prudence Johnson's.

Brabbin explained. 'They like to make you sweat first. That's almost as enjoyable as taking your scalp, ma'am.'

Prudence Johnson's hand shot to her tight bun of mousy hair, holding on to it tightly.

'Really, sir,' Hanley protested. 'Have you no consideration at all for the ladies' feelings?'

'Only answering Miss Johnson's question,' Brabbin drawled.

The gambler let his eyes wander over the

passengers, and he'd be damned if he could see in any of them the threat that he was on board to defeat. Which one was he after? Stradden? Who had flogged a Negro almost to death for stealing a bowl of soup from his kitchen. Prudence Johnson? A woman vibrant with hatred, who used the Good Book as a weapon of war instead of an instrument of peace, an advocate of racial purity, Kate Branigan? The *Bell Creek Sentinel*'s stand on the governor's plans for equality for Negroes and Indians with whites had been virulent opposition, advocating that the lands won from the Indians should be the preserve of the whiteman, and that Negroes should be confined to the South where they belonged. The newspaper's stand was a popular one. There was hardly a man or woman in Bell Creek who had not lost a loved one as the settlers had pushed West, and feelings were still raw. Where did Kate Branigan stand? Did she fully support the *Sentinel*'s firebrand editorials? Or was she simply earning a crust?

Brabbin's keen grey eyes travelled on to the pale, wispy-haired Walter Hanley. His eyes came to rest on the long, tapering, work-shy fingers, which did not seem to have the strength in them to pull a trigger. There was little or nothing about Hanley in the brief passed to him in jail. That left Gertrude Bletchley, described in the brief as kindly and passive of nature. He reckoned he could safely discount her – Luther Sheriff

Spencer, too. The Bell Creek sheriff was a highly respected lawman.

It was hard to imagine any of his fellow passengers as an assassin. But one of them surely was. Which one?

Ace Brabbin's mind drifted back three weeks to a meeting with the territorial governor . . .

THREE

'Sit down, Mr Brabbin.' The governor introduced the other man at the meeting. 'This is my aide, Ron Abbot.' Brabbin took Abbot's hand, and found his handshake cold and disapproving. 'He's got some disturbing news, I'm afraid. Ron.'

Abbot, a gaunt-framed man with a matching hollow voice began:

'News has reached us, Mr Brabbin, that an attempt to assassinate the governor will be made in a town called Cheyney, where he will be delivering an important speech in a couple of weeks' time. As you probably are aware, sir, the governor plans to introduce legislation to give equality to Negroes and Indians with whitefolk.'

Brabbin reckoned, by Abbot's stance, that it was an idea he fully supported

'Of course, such forward thinking on the governor's part has not met with approval in some

27

quarters. Indeed, some are stridently opposed to such integration at this time.'

Brabbin concluded, based on Abbot's pointed stating of the governor's intentions, that he could likely be included in those against or cautious to such a radical move.

Abbot continued:

'The Civil War has left many open wounds – as indeed have the Indian wars. There are many Southerners unable to come to terms with the Confederacy's defeat, and are hoping one day soon to reverse the Union victory.

'The governor's personal commitment to fairness and equality as being the only sensible way forward for this territory to heal its wounds, become prosperous, and combat the rising tide of lawlessness invoked by the divisions that exist, is absolute and unwavering.

'Of course, there are opponents to the governor's plans for a bill of rights for the Indians and Negroes right here in camp, too.'

The acrimonious wrangling between the governor and some members of the legislature had been well documented in the press.

Abbot said: 'But, while argument is one thing, assassination is an intolerable and unacceptable blow to our fledgling territory, and must be stopped, sir.'

'I want you to find this assassin, Mr Brabbin,' the governor said. 'Before his bullet finds me.'

Ron Abbot said: 'Our information is, that the assassin will travel on the stage from Bell Creek to Cheyney on the day before the governor is due to make his speech.'

'I want you to be on that stage, Mr Brabbin,' the governor said. 'I'll be depending on you to unmask this cur.'

'Any idea what this man looks like?' Brabbin had asked.

Abbot shook his head. 'The assassin may not even be a man, Mr Brabbin.'

Ace Brabbin's mind drifted back further, before his visit to the governor, when, in a flea-pit hotel hugging the Mex border, Colonel John Stewart, the former head of the Confederate Secret Service in which Brabbin had been an agent, was waiting for him when he returned from the card-tables. Stewart was now serving the Union in a similar role.

'A good night, Robert?' Stewart had enquired.

The appellation of Ace had come in more recent times, earned at the gambling-tables in saloons and along the Mississippi on the paddle-steamers. He had not been called Robert in a long time.

'Beans and jerky takings,' Brabbin had told Stewart, once he'd gotten over his surprise at seeing his former commanding officer.

'How have you been doing, Robert?' John Stewart enquired kindly.

'I've been getting by.'

It was something a whole lot of Southerners who had moved West after the Confederacy's defeat could not claim. He had been luckier than most. Having always had a natural skill with cards, he had become a gambler. Not the most auspicious career a man could take up, but, Brabbin had reasoned, logically, that knowing only how to grow cotton, soldier and play cards, if he needed to eat it had to be cards. Maybe in time he would return to soldiering. But right then he was not ready to don the blue of the Union, having first to cleanse his mind of the Confederacy's defeat.

'Got a desk job in Washington now,' Stewart informed Brabbin. He slapped his right leg, mangled by cannon fire in the last days of the war. 'Active soldiering was out of the question.'

Brabbin was not quick enough to cover up his surprise and indeed sense of betrayal at the colonel's having joined what, to many Southerners, was still the enemy. It would take a long time for the festering wounds of conflict to heal, and longer still for the gall of defeat to be swallowed.

Stewart's response to Brabbin's reaction was bitter-sweet.

'I wish the South had won the war, Robert. But it did not. And this great country now has to forget the war's legacy and forge ahead to the future. Looking back won't change anything.'

Ace Brabbin realized that his silent condemnation of his former commanding officer was grudging. A lot of Southerners had done as John Stewart had done; accepting defeat and embracing the new order, sick and tired of war. Some became bitter; some indifferent. Others took to drifting as he had. Men had hired out the killing-skills they had honed on the battlefields. Some, too, had killing in their blood, and knew no other way to resolve a conflict other than by a gun. He had used a gun, but he had not grown to love it as others had. Of necessity, in the profession he had chosen, he had to be fast. And it troubled him sometimes how comfortable a sixgun felt in his hand.

'I guess not,' Brabbin said in answer to Stewart's mild rebuke about looking back solving nothing.

'Do you remember my brother Daniel?' Stewart had asked.

Brabbin had laughed. 'Guess I'll never forget.'

Brabbin remembered his gaping surprise on first being introduced to Daniel Stewart, a Confederate captain, just before Shiloh. Daniel Stewart and his older brother John were as unlike brothers in appearance and manner as a mountain cat and a rabbit. Daniel was diminutive, about five foot four, to John's six foot three. And while John Stewart had strong, jutting features, with mellow eyes, Daniel Stewart had a porcelain,

almost feminine face, with darting, button blue
eyes. Daniel Stewart was spiteful and spitting, his
brother considerate and caring. Brabbin recalled
being surprised to find that both men came from
the same womb.

'Daniel never could accept the South's surren-
der. He frowns on my working for the Union. It
pains me that the war should have caused men
who were formerly bonded by the grey and by
blood now to be so at odds with each other.'

'I guess it isn't that hard to understand,
Colonel,' Brabbin reasoned. 'There were a lot of
men who were willing to fight to the last man,
rather than see a Union flag hoisted in the South.
On the evidence of my short acquaintance with
your brother Daniel, he was one of those men.'

'And you, Robert?' John Stewart asked. 'Would
you have fought on to the last man standing? You
never did let a man into your thoughts much.'

'I don't know if I have an answer to that question, Colonel. And I've given up asking myself.
These days I turn a card and make a dollar, and
never count on doing the same tomorrow.'
Reflectively, he said: 'If it's one thing the war
taught me, it was never to count your tomorrows.
They may not come.'

'Drink?' Stewart invited, taking a silver hip-
flask from his pocket. 'Kentucky rye.'

Brabbin took the flask and drank liberally,
relishing the smooth, rich liquor, his palate these

days being more tuned to the rot-gut the Western saloons served up as liquor. Handing back the flask, he chuckled. 'When it comes to good liquor the South can claim victory, Colonel.'

Fencing over with, Brabbin asked the question that had been burning a hole in his tongue since he'd set eyes on John Stewart.

'Why have you sought me out, Colonel?'

Stewart smiled. 'Can't a man visit with a former comrade, Robert?'

Not ever a man patient with shadow-boxing. Brabbin said: 'Colonel, we're a couple of miles from the Mex border. In a town you could buy with a pound of dog shit. In a hotel that one day soon will walk away on the backs of its bugs.'

His level gaze rested on Stewart.

'So, I'll ask you again, sir. Why did you seek me out?'

'The governor would like to see you, Robert.'

Brabbin was stunned. 'The governor?'

'Yes.'

'On what business?'

'His personal safety,' Stewart had informed him. Ace Brabbin was lost for words. Stewart went on:

'You were the best intelligence officer the South had, and the one the Yankees feared and admired most. You weren't nicknamed the Grey Ghost for nothing, Robert. When the question of the governor's safety came up, your name came up, too.'

Brabbin said wryly: 'That would have me working for the Union, Colonel.'

'Yes, it would,' Stewart stated flatly. 'And I'll understand if you find that action a bridge too far, Robert. But perhaps if you talk to the governor himself . . .'.

The stage lurched dangerously as its right-sided wheels became caught up in a rut where the trail had been washed away by recent rains. The sudden heaving of the stage jerked Ace Brabbin out of his reverie, and he became aware again of his fellow-passengers, all of whom were worried to a lesser or greater degree by the attention the Apaches were giving the stage. They had come nearer, pacing the stage as it headed for a canyon up ahead, through which it would have to pass to reach the relay station at Indian Creek, where a change of horses was due.

Walter Hanley said: 'It's crazy to go through that canyon. We could be boxed in and slaughtered.'

It was a worry shared by Sheriff Spencer. And it was a horror too terrifying for Prudence Johnson to contemplate. Her head was filled with the lurid stories about Indians and their fondness for white women.

Gertrude Bletchley added her concerns to the discussion.

'What do you think, Ace?' Kate asked the gambler.

'I figure the canyon could give us problems.'

'How do you figure that?' Spencer asked. 'They're a-ways behind, and it's a short canyon. I reckon we could outrun them.'

Brabbin said: 'Where there's one Apache, there's more. Maybe right in the rocks of that canyon.'

'Yes indeed,' Prudence Johnson said, her voice wild with hysteria. 'Those savages are totally unpredictable.'

'Don't know why they're holding off,' Hanley said. 'But that's what they're doing sure enough. If they had wanted to, they could have had every scalp on this stage by now.'

'Why would they want to hold off attacking the stage?' The question was Kate Branigan's.

Brabbin shrugged. 'They have their reasons, of that you can be sure.'

'What kind of reason would that be?' Luther Spencer asked.

'A friend on board, maybe?'

Brabbin's answer stirred a hornets' nest of indignation.

'How dare you, sir?' Prudence Johnson wailed.

'That's pretty low thinking in my book, Brabbin,' Stradden growled.

'If anyone else has got any other suggestion as to why they are attack-shy, then state it,' the

35

gambler challenged.

No one did.

Brabbin elaborated on his theory.

'I hear tell that some of the bucks have repeater rifles. Not many. But some.'

'And?' Amos Stradden snapped.

'Where did they get them?'

Hanley said: 'Gunrunners?'

'They sure didn't buy them at the general store,' Brabbin said.

'And you think the agent who supplied these repeaters is on board this stage?' Kate Branigan asked.

'What you're suggesting is monstrous,' Prudence Johnson told Brabbin. 'The folk on this stage are decent folk.' Her voice became as chilly as arctic ice. 'That is, except you, Mr Brabbin. Running guns to the Indians might just be the kind of thing you'd do, I dare say!'

'Folk aren't always what they seem to be, Miss Johnson,' Brabbin said quietly. 'Who knows what's in a body's heart and mind?'

'Rubbish!' Stradden dismissed stridently.

'Never take a book by the cover, eh?' Kate Branigan said.

'Yes, ma'am,' Ace Brabbin answered. His gaze travelled to the diminutive Gertrude Bletchley, huddled in the far corner of the stage. 'Do you have a view on all of this, ma'am?' he enquired.

The old woman's delicately proportioned

features broke in a smile, and the bright-as-button blue eyes looked steadily at Brabbin. 'At my time of life, Mr Brabbin,' she said, in a delicate voice, 'fretting and speculating is just a waste of time.'

'Aren't you scared of the Apaches?' Prudence Johnson asked. 'You're a woman.'

The little old woman laughed. 'I'm a prune, Miss Johnson. Of no use, even to an Indian.'

Walter Hanley said: 'I still think we should avoid the canyon. There must be another way.'

Spencer pronounced: 'South of the canyon is sandy, the stage would surely bog down. And the west trail hasn't been used in a long time because of rock slides. Might even be boulder-strewn and impassable. Don't see we have any choice but to head through the canyon, and hope we'll reach Indian Creek ahead of those savages.'

'We could head north to Banyon?' Brabbin suggested.

'Banyon is a damn ghost town,' Stradden bellowed stridently.

Luther Spencer quickly backed the rancher. 'Banyon will take us away from Indian Creek.'

Kate Branigan said: 'Might be better than risking the canyon. If we could hold out, help might come. There must be troopers out looking for the renegades.'

Prudence Johnson came down on Kate's side.

Brabbin said: 'There's a hill trail out of Banyon

to Indian Creek relay station. We'd arrive a little late, but maybe with our skins intact.'

Stradden doused the gambler's plan.

'You're spouting rubbish, Brabbin. Best we risk the canyon, than go haring off all over the country. Why, that hill trail out of Banyon is nothing more than a rutted mule-track now.'

'How do you know that?' the gambler asked in a quiet tone.

Stradden swung about on Brabbin, flustered. 'It must be. It wasn't much more than a mule-track to begin with. And with prospecting long gone in the hills. Well . . .'

It was sound reasoning, Brabbin decided. Yet, he was certain that Stradden's information about the state of repair of the hill trail from Banyon to Indian Creek was based on recent knowledge, rather than speculative assumption. But if that were so, why would he not admit as much?

'Do we have any other choice but to head for Banyon?' Kate Branigan pondered.

'Once we reach Banyon – if we reach Banyon,' Stradden corrected, blustering, 'will our position be any better in a desert ghost town?'

Walter Hanley opined: 'A whole lot better than being sitting targets from the high reaches of the canyon. And what if those bastards box us in?'

'Why don't we take a vote?' Kate Branigan sensibly suggested.

Luther Spencer dithered in his support for Kate's

solution, while Stradden's opposition became even more resolute and strident. Hanley was in favour – Prudence Johnson, too. Gertrude Bletchley, on the other hand, fully supported the rancher's argument for making a break through the canyon.

'It's my niece, Emma, you see. She'll be waiting for me in Cheyney,' was her reason for risking the canyon. 'She'll worry so if I don't arrive on time. She's not well.'

'Ace?' Kate asked.

'Killers don't get a vote, Miss Branigan,' Stradden growled.

'Don't see why not,' the *Bell Creek Sentinel* reporter countered. 'His scalp is at risk too.'

Spencer said: 'Ain't it up to the Fargo crew to make the decision anyway?'

Stradden shot the sheriff a keenly hostile look. 'We're the passengers, Luther. We'll be the ones to decide what's best for us.'

The impasse was becoming increasingly ill-tempered and thorny.

Gertrude Bletchley again reminded everyone of her need to get to Cheyney as scheduled. 'Poor Emma will fret so if I don't show up.'

Brabbin again had a feeling of having met the diminutive Miss Bletchley before.

The flustered Amos Stradden showed disregard for the old lady's feelings. 'Your niece will have something real to gripe about if your bones instead of your person arrives.'

39

The rancher earned resounding condemnation for his uncaring attitude.

Prudence Johnson, becoming more and more distressed with the threat from outside and the increasingly acrimonious exchanges inside the coach, pleaded, 'Let's take a vote, as Miss Branigan suggested.'

The stage passengers divided evenly. Three for Banyon. Three for racing through the canyon. Those for Banyon were Prudence Johnson, Kate Branigan and Walter Hanley. Spencer sided with Stradden, though against his better judgement, Brabbin felt. Miss Bletchley became the third advocate of racing through the canyon.

'That leaves us tied,' said Kate. 'Looks like Mr Brabbin will have the deciding vote.'

'The hell he will,' the sheriff chanted.

'What else can we do?' Kate reasoned.

'We've got to make up our minds,' Prudence Johnson fretted.

Kate said: 'Either someone changes their vote, or . . .'

Walter Hanley said: 'Let Brabbin have his say.'

'The say-so of a murderer decides our fate?' Stradden shook his head violently. 'That's the craziest thing I've ever heard.'

The arguments and counter arguments began all over again, until Kate Branigan frustratedly declared:

'Well, you decide, Sheriff. You're the law.'

Luther Spencer clearly hated the quandary in which the *Sentinel* reporter had placed him.

'Well,' the rancher prodded the sheriff, 'what's it to be, Luther?'

The men locked eyes, Stradden's the more dominant. His displeasure was glaring when Spencer opted for Banyon.

'I guess it'll be safer than risking the canyon,' he explained to Stradden.

But Ace Brabbin reckoned that the lawman's explanation was more an apology than an explanation. Why?

Stradden argued the toss tigerishly.

Ace Brabbin's gaze took in the band of pacing Indians, who had grown in number as more bucks filtered down from the ridges to join the original war party.

'Better make up your minds. And pretty fast, too,' the gambler advised.

'Banyon it is,' Spencer declared defiantly.

Brabbin noted that the lawman's defiance was directed exclusively at Stradden.

FOUR

Brabbin's mind drifted to the possibility that the assassin might be a woman. He had only known one female assassin. It was the wisdom that women were not assassins. But then, like every place else, the West was changing. Rumours about women running for political office and agitating for what they called *women's rights* were filtering through from the big cities. Unthinkable goings-on. He considered the women on board the stage. Kate Branigan was fiery enough, but seemed too well-balanced to fit the profile of an assassin. Prudence Johnson, on the other hand, was beset by many conflicts which could make her the kind of disaffected person who would fit perfectly an assassin's profile.

And what about the delicate, mild mannered, Gertrude Bletchley? An assassin? Brabbin reckoned not.

Ron Abbot had stepped in to tell many hair-raising tales about women of intrigue down the centuries, finishing with the warning:

'For the governor's safety, we've got to cover all possibilities, Mr Brabbin.' Abbot had raised an eyebrow, and had asked starchily in response to the gambler's laughter, 'Did I say something that amuses you, sir?'

Brabbin had replied: 'Well, doesn't it seem strange to you, Mr Abbot? Governor? That you should be handing this task to a Reb?'

Abbot was blunt in his response. 'You wouldn't be my choice, Brabbin.'

The card-player glanced to the governor. 'And you, Governor?'

'I can't say that I'm entirely happy having my life in the hands of a Reb, sir,' he replied honestly.

'But John Stewart, and this . . . ' He took a thick file from his desk-drawer and held it aloft before slamming it down on his desk, 'a record of your undercover exploits against the Union during the war, have convinced me that the best man is on the job.'

The hefty volume's title was: *The Grey Ghost*.

The argument about heading for Indian Creek relay station via the hill trail from Banyon was decided. The decision was conveyed to the Fargo driver, who, blessedly, agreed with heading for the ghost town without further disagreement.

Lew Crowley, the shotgun rider, was not as friendly to the idea.

'Banyon?' he yelped. 'There's nothin' there but a clutch of rottin' buildings. 'Sides, the nags are 'bout done for. We should be makin' tracks for Indian Creek instead of gallivantin' 'round the country, Andy.'

'The horses are spent?' Prudence Johnson wailed.

Andy Wright had been keeping that worry to himself. The story of the horses' tiredness could be read in the reins, and it was a tale that could have a very abrupt ending. The two lead horses had been replaced at the station east of Bell Creek, but due to a livery fire the other horses could not be changed. So that made for two relatively spritely animals, and four tired ones. Not a good combination. Any one of the four could give up the ghost any time. Particularly if they had to outrun an Indian attack. Even pacing the two spritelier beasts was testing their stamina to the limit.

It would only be with hindsight that they would be able to judge the wisdom of the decision taken. Andy Wright pointed the Concord towards Banyon.

'I figure,' Lew Crowley opined, 'that we're goin' to find trouble with a capital T!'

FIVE

'Mightn't even be a trail headed that way now,' Crowley said, continuing his gripe. 'Banyon's been dust for years.'

'I reckon Brabbin's called it right, Lew,' said Andy Wright. 'It's flat, open country 'tween here and Banyon. Nowhere for an Apache ambush. And we'll have clear targets from the stage to shoot at if they attack us.'

'Are you takin' advice from a killer now, Andy?' Lew Crowley asked, sourly. 'That gambler's prob'ly got his own reasons for wantin' to head for Banyon. Longer he takes to reach Cheyney, longer he'll keep his neck out of a noose. I say we go arrow-straight through the canyon.'

Stradden, picking up on Crowley's dissent, revived his argument for avoiding Banyon. The new round of disagreement reached Andy Wright.

'Wish you folk would make up your minds,' the driver shouted testily.

'The sheriff's decided on Banyon, Mr Stradden,' Kate Branigan said.

Kate's reminder earned the lawman a spiteful look from the rancher, and he said soulfully: 'Yeah, he did, didn't he.'

Brabbin got the distinct impression that within the arguments raging back and forth across the stage, Stradden's and the sheriff's was a personal one. Brabbin wondered why that should be.

Goaded, Spencer stepped back into the picture. He poked his head out of the window. 'Keep heading for Banyon, Andy,' he ordered. 'On my say-so as a lawman.'

The sheriff's word was good enough for Andy Wright, a strong supporter of law and order.

'Banyon, it is.'

The Concord creaked and groaned, every rivet and joint straining as Wright cut as fast a trail for the ghost town as the tired team could muster, his whip curling and unfurling over the hind quarters of the horses to urge them to maximum effort.

The stage's swift change of direction caught the Apaches by surprise. Their anger flared at being duped, Wright having opened up a sizeable gap in the couple of minutes it took the Apache bucks to realize that the stage was veering away from the canyon. But those lost minutes were quickly retrieved. They galloped full-out after the stage, the air filled with their war cries.

Luckily, the bucks were short of repeater rifles, with only one or two showing. The rest had to make do with old carbines that were as likely to blow up in their faces as cause any mayhem to the stage passengers. Arrows, though, were in plentiful supply and were raining down on the stage, thudding into the aged Concord which was well past its glory days. One arrow passed through the passenger compartment and straight out the opposite window; it was fortunate for the group that it did not find a softer target than the rotten cottonwood it did find.

Stradden and Spencer were on their knees covering the left-side door. Hanley was shooting an old Dragoon Colt from the opposite window, overcoming the fickleness of the aged weapon to pick his targets at will. In fact, Ace Brabbin had seldom seen a shooter of such accuracy and quality from a bucking stage. It made him see Walter Hanley in a new light. The gambler concluded that Hanley's gun prowess might very well be the kind that an assassin would need.

Kate Branigan was shooting with spirit as well, downing a duo of Indians who had raced up alongside the stage to try and swing aboard. Prudence Johnson sat huddled in the corner wailing – Brabbin, straining his rawhide ligature, caught her by the ankles and dragged her to the floor.

'How dare you!' she rebuked him.

'Stay down,' Brabbin said harshly, dragging her

back down as she attempted to regain her seat. 'It's safer down here.'

'I have no intention, irrespective of what danger I might be in, to lie alongside you on this floor, Mr Brabbin!' she spat. An arrow flew through the window and thudded into the seat where Prudence Johnson had been sitting. Her wailing became even louder, and she leapt up, tearing at her hair. 'I can't stand another second of this,' she cried out, and threw open the stage door to jump free.

A snarling Apache filled the open door, reaching for Prudence Johnson. Brabbin's boot shot out to kick the Indian in the groin, just as his hand grabbed Prudence Johnson's hair. The Apache, his face crimped with the ferocious pain that Ace Brabbin's boot had inflicted on him, tried in vain to retain his grip on the rail of the stage's roof-rack. Brabbin's leg shot out again to punish the Indian further. This time, with a howl out of the depths of hell, he lost his grip. The stage rocked and shuddered as its speeding wheels mangled the Indian.

Prudence Johnson collapsed in a heap.

Kate Branigan's mothering instincts came to the fore and she deserted her post to tend to Johnson.

'Stay where you are, Kate!' Brabbin ordered. 'Plenty of time for nursing once we're free of the threat of losing our hair.' He shouted at Spencer.

'Cut me loose and give me a damn gun, Sheriff!'

Spencer did not dither. He sliced through the gambler's rawhide bonds and granted his request.

'Are you crazy, Spencer?' Stradden protested. 'Handing a gun to a killer.'

Spencer concluded reasonably. 'Don't see that I have a choice, Stradden. Way I see it, Brabbin will be much too busy saving his scalp. And to have a chance of surviving those savages' onslaught, we need ev'ry man who can shoot, shooting.'

Brabbin shoved the .45 in the waistband of his trousers. 'Cover me,' he ordered Hanley. He flung open the stage door, and grabbed the rail of the roof luggage-rack to haul himself on to the roof where he knew Stradden's and the sheriff's rifles to be.

The boom of the shotgun rider's Greener was rolling across the flat plain. A pair of bucks were shredded and blasted from their ponies. The other renegades immediately gave the Greener the respect it demanded, and fell back out of its wide and deadly range. Brabbin, belly-flat on the Concord's roof, grabbed a rifle. The Apache was a crafty opponent. They had fanned out, weaving and dodging, buying time to change tactics. When they did, they offered Lew Crowley a wide range of targets, coming at the stage from several directions at once, even offering some bucks up to his blunderbuss to allow others to skip through the gaps. The strategy worked well, and with every passing second the war party were gaining the upper hand. Ace Brabbin didn't waste a bullet. Each time his repeater spat, there was another riderless Apache pony. The guns inside the stage were also taking their toll, as was Crowley's shotgun. But all Brabbin had was the ammunition in the rifles, and that was soon spent. The sporadic shooting from the stage itself was evidence, too, of the dwindling supply of bullets. Realizing their plight, more and more bucks were eager to gain glory by being first to board the stage.

The sound of empty gun chambers became the norm.

'Our goose is cooked,' Lew Crowley opined. 'Should've gone for the canyon, Andy.'

Ace Brabbin shared Crowley's glum view of the outcome.

SIX

A sudden lurch of the Concord swept Brabbin into space. His arm was almost wrenched from its socket. He fought the blinding pain to retain his hold on the luggage-rack rail. Before he had time to adjust to the sudden emergency, the stage swerved to the opposite side of the trail and swung him back to smash him against the Concord before he could get his legs up to ward off the bone-jarring impact. The wind whooshed from his lungs and his eyes danced, distorting his vision. A tomahawk whizzed past and embedded itself in the stage just inches away from the gambler's head; a pair of arrows quickly followed. This time the vagaries of the trail worked to his advantage. The stage rolled. The arrows flew harmlessly over the wildly swaying Concord. However, though the stage's roll had been fortunate, it also worked against Brabbin, piling pain on pain as he fought to keep his grip on the roof-rail. He could not maintain his hold for much longer. A weariness was creeping up his arm. Gritting his teeth, he mustered his last reserves of strength to haul himself back on to the roof.

One of the bucks had got within striking distance of Brabbin. Kate Branigan's accurate shot saved his skull from being opened by the Apache's swinging tomahawk. Brabbin grinned through his pain.

'Thanks, Kate.'

Kate returned his smile and said: 'I guess you've got gambler's luck, Ace. That was my last bullet.'

The snap of bolts separating from wood as the roof-rail yielded to his weight, alerted Brabbin to impending danger.

'Thing is,' the gambler observed, 'luck has to run out some time, Kate.'

Another bolt popped.

'Like right now for example.'

Brabbin knew that he had only seconds before all the rivets securing the rail popped from their sockets in turn. He was faced with death under the stage wheels. Or death at the hands of the Apache.

'Some choice,' he muttered.

'We need help here!' Kate announced, as she grappled with Brabbin.

Sheriff Spencer, having the brawn that Hanley did not have, and the muscle which in Amos

Stradden had turned to flab with the easy living that a man of his considerable wealth had, hurried to Kate's assistance. He grabbed Brabbin around the knees and held him, as the gambler secured his hold on the crumbling rail and clawed his way upwards with Lew Crowley's help. Andy Wright, straining to control the excited team and keep them on as even a keel as possible, shouted out a warning to Brabbin:

'Gap up ahead!'

Ace Brabbin glanced over his shoulder to the narrow gap the stage would be hurtling through in seconds, with only an inch or two to spare. He paled on seeing the jagged boulder that was tilting like a Saturday night drunk at the opening to the gap. He scrambled to gain the stage roof. If he did not make it, he would be torn to shreds for sure by the jagged boulder.

SEVEN

Brabbin heaved himself on to the stage roof with a split-second to spare, before a hunk of rock as sharp as a shark's tooth tore a ragged hole in the Concord's side, just above the door and under the roof, leaving a yawning gap that could prove deadly to the passengers' well being. The rail gave up the ghost and shattered, sending shards of wood, some as pointed as a dagger, buzzing around the gambler's head – luckily, none causing him injury. Lew Crowley was not as fortunate. One spinning fragment of the rail dug deep into his arm to slice away the flesh and expose the bone. The accident had rendered the shotgun rider redundant as a defender. There was no way that he could use the Greener. Brabbin could exchange his sixgun for the shotgun, but whatever chance there would be to line up a target from inside the stage, any sixgun action from the

54

roof of the stage to bag an Apache, would need a lot more luck than was presently their lot.

Brabbin tore a strip from his shirt and made a tourniquet to stem the rapid loss of blood from Crowley's wound. Urgently he looked to the gaining Apaches, now more or less enjoying a trouble-free assault on the stage. Low on ammunition, the stage passengers could only now pick their targets with care, having to make every bullet count.

To add to their misfortune, the stage's left-side rear wheel had mounted a rock on its hair-raising passage through the gap, which had buckled its rim, making the stage virtually out of control as it swayed and rolled. Any concerted response to the Apache attack was near impossible. The stage was slowing too.

'This team is all tuckered out,' Andy Wright warned Brabbin. 'And I reckon that in no time at all, if we keep pushin' like this, that back wheel is goin' to shatter.' He added bad news to bad news. 'Some of the team'll prob'ly drop as well.'

'I darn well knew we should've headed through the canyon,' Crowley again groused.

Misfortune piled on misfortune as the stage hit a patch of sandy soil and its wheels bogged down. To keep rolling and pull clear of the sucking soil, Wright had to use his whip mercilessly on the team. A middle horse almost lost its footing. With luck, and no small measure of skill, the Fargo driver checked the horse's stumble, and the team forged ahead.

'That was one last effort,' Wright opined. 'Their wind is gone.'

Brabbin was beginning to think that maybe it was their fate to die at the hands of the Apaches.

'It's another coupla miles to this Banyon burg,' Lew Crowley shouted above the clatter of the disintegrating Concord. 'About two miles from that twist in the trail ahead.'

'I figure we'll make it,' Brabbin said.

Wright's despondent shake of his head contradicted that view.

Ace Brabbin's eyes widened on seeing the cruel, savage face appearing over the rear of the stage, a knife between his teeth. Brabbin pulled the Colt. The pistol's hammer snagged on the waistband of his trousers. He quickly improvised and hurled a suitcase with the initials K.B. engraved on it at the Indian. It wasn't much of a weapon, but Brabbin's aim was accurate. The hard leather case caught the Indian on the crown of his head, doing enough to unsettle him. The gambler grabbed the hunting-knife in Lew Crowley's belt and slung it. The blade became embedded in the Indian's throat. It opened up a jagged wound, and sliced through his windpipe. He dropped out of sight with a blood-curdling scream. The suitcase had sprung open and Kate Branigan's clothing was swept away. All except a pair of red silk bloomers, which snagged on the rear of the stage. They blew in the wind like a battle flag. Brabbin grappled with a second Indian who leaped on to the stage. A third Apache appeared. Brabbin faced a double threat. Andy Wright came to his rescue. He flicked out his whip to snare one of the Indian's feet, and tugged fiercely on the whip. It uncoiled and tossed the Indian off the stage. He fell on his head and his neck snapped. Brabbin then grabbed the whip and looped it around the other renegade's neck and viciously tightened the makeshift garrotte, until the Apache went limp. He tossed him off the Concord.

From the foothills to the left of the trail more Indians joined the attack led by, Ace Brabbin guessed, the blood thirsty and merciless Blood Wing.

You'll be travelling a deadly trail, Brabbin.

The governor's words came winging back to the gambler. He muttered: 'You sure got that right, Governor.'

'We're done for!' Andy Wright spat angrily.

Almost out of ammunition. On board a stage coming apart at the seams. Drawn by nags on their last legs. Surrounded by howling Apaches . . .

Brabbin figured the Fargo driver's assessment was on the nose.

EIGHT

Wave after wave of marauding Apaches swept in on the slowing stage. The Concord was dotted with arrows, sliced by lances, and punctured by tomahawks. The Indians, too, were proving no mean shots, leaving the stage peppered with holes. It was an outright miracle that, as yet, passengers and crew had not suffered any casualties except for cuts and abrasions.

But how long could their luck last?

Blood Wing, sensing victory, swept in to lead the attack.

'What the hell do you think you're doing, Stradden?'

Walter Hanley, who had asked the astonished question, watched with the other passengers in amazement as the rancher kicked open the Concord door, with the clear intention of joining Ace Brabbin on the roof of the crazily bucking stage.

'You'll be cut to pieces,' Luther Spencer warned the rancher.

But there was no diverting Stradden from his lunatic gamble.

'Give me your hand,' the rancher shouted to Brabbin.

The gambler leaned over the side and hauled Stradden on to the roof, while landing a boot in the face of a buck with a lance who was intent on severing Stradden's spine. Both men lay flat on the roof with arrows whizzing past.

Brabbin said: 'That was a loco thing to do.'

'I didn't want to die inside that damn box,' the rancher growled.

Stradden piled amazement on amazement. He got to his knees and ordered Brabbin: 'Grab my legs. I damn well want to see my killers face to face.'

Incredulously, he stood up, swaying dangerously, Brabbin straining every muscle to keep him from being pitched off the stage. Incredulity was stretched to breaking point when Blood Wing called off his attack.

Stradden cut loose with a wild, delighted whoop. 'I didn't think I looked that ugly, dammit.'

Andy Wright, a much relieved man, hauled the team back to a steady pace, coaxing and cajoling the animals out of their fright until they calmed and settled. With the threat from the Apaches miraculously in abeyance, he let them slow to an amble, and then to a halt.

'Best if you sit the rest of this ride out inside the coach, Lew,' he told the shotgun rider, and got back a feisty rebuff from Crowley:

'I started as the shotgun, Andy. And I'll damn well finish as the shotgun!'

'It's good advice that Andy is handing out,' was Ace Brabbin's opinion.

'I ain't askin' you for yer opinion, gambler,' Crowley spat.

Brabbin, tired and riled, was in no humour to gasbag with the shotgun rider. He told him bluntly, 'You're weak from loss of blood, all tuckered out, and about as useful right now as a castrated man in a cathouse, Crowley.'

The shotgun rider flinched, but did not let go of his protest.

'You got no say, Brabbin. You ain't a Fargo man.'

'Don't want you topplin' off the box and breakin' ev'ry bone in your body, Lew,' Wright said kindly.

'We ain't outa the woods yet,' Crowley growled. 'You need a shotgun if'n them 'Paches change their minds, Andy. Or maybe you'll cross trails with road agents, ever think of that?'

'I'll ride shotgun,' Ace Brabbin volunteered.

'You're a gambler,' Lew Crowley flung back, his opinion of the profession and its practitioners unambiguous. 'What d'ya know 'bout bein' a shotgun rider?'

Brabbin picked up the Greener from the end of the box, broke it to check its loads, then pointed and pulled. A rock balancing on a boulder a distance away to the side of the trail shattered under the shotgun's blast.

'Hah!' Crowley sneered, though clearly impressed. 'That's a good-sized rock.'

Brabbin repeated his shooting feat, this time selecting a rock less than half the size of the original with equally devastating effect.

'Guess you can handle a blunderbuss sure 'nuff,' Crowley grudgingly conceded.

Alighting from the stage, Spencer said: 'Mr Brabbin is mighty handy with any kind of shooting-iron – too handy.' He ordered the gambler back inside the stage. 'Where I can keep an eye on you.'

Amos Stradden took up the role of shotgun rider.

'Don't have the kind of shooting skills that Brabbin's got. But all a fella's got to do with this beauty,' he cradled the Greener in his arms, 'is point and pull, and everything vanishes.'

Not taking kindly to any lessening of his role, Lew Crowley crowed. 'It's dunderhead thinkin' like that Stradden, that makes a Greener dangerous. You gotta respect a shotgun as much as a good woman. Or like a good woman, if misused, will turn agin ya when ya needs it most.'

'Down,' Spencer ordered Brabbin, sixgun cocked. When the gambler's feet touched ground, the sheriff stepped to one side to cover him. He asked Hanley, 'I'd be obliged if you'd bind his hands, sir.' The lawman held out several strips of rawhide with the instruction, 'Loop them into one.'

Hanley was eager to oblige, diligently inter-twining the strips of rawhide. He stretched them until they made an unbreakable bond.

'Ace risked his life, Sheriff,' Kate Branigan protested. 'Seems mighty ungrateful that he should be treated like a common crim—'

She bit off her words.

'That's what he is, ma'am,' Spencer said, 'a common criminal. And I can't take chances with you folks' well being.'

Kate reminded the lawman: 'He had a gun in his hand. He didn't use it on any of us.'

Walter Hanley scoffed. 'He was much too busy trying to save his own hide. Now it's different.'

'Where could he escape to?' Kate countered. 'He'd ride straight into Apache fury. Which would be no escape at all.'

'I think that Mr Brabbin, being a killer, should not be free to cause mayhem, Sheriff.'

All eyes went to Gertrude Bletchley, sitting calmly unruffled where she had been before the Indian attack. Her bright button eyes met Brabbin's with a steady, challenging gaze; eyes which he was sure he had looked into before. But how could that be? He had never set eyes on Gertrude Bletchley before he had made her acquaintance on the stage.

Support for Brabbin came from the most unlikely source of all – Prudence Johnson.

'Though I did at first, I don't now believe that Mr Brabbin is a threat, Sheriff Spencer. I agree with Miss Branigan that shackling Mr Brabbin is indeed a poor repayment for his heroic efforts in fighting off those savages.'

Walter Hanley said spitefully: 'He did nothing that I could see, except get out of the stage. Did he even fire one shot in anger, driver?' he quizzed Andy Wright.

'He killed one of those bastards as he tried to board the stage from the rear,' said Wright. 'If that 'Pache had got on board—'

'I'd venture to say that in so doing, saving his own scalp was Brabbin's primary motivation,' Walter Hanley scoffingly interjected. 'Would that be right, sir?' he enquired of the Fargo driver.

Wright's response was spiky. 'Ain't that what ev'ryone was doin'?'

Hanley scowled furiously, having expected a resounding endorsement of his views from the driver. His scowl intensified as Wright added:

'Just as Brabbin climbed topside, Lew was wounded and bleedin' somethin' awful. He would prob'ly have taken a dive if Brabbin hadn't been there to help out.'

As the sheriff weighed the arguments for and against shackling Brabbin, Ron Abbot's owl-wise words echoed in the gambler's mind:

In my experience, Mr Brabbin, a friend by day is often an enemy by night.

Why had Prudence Johnson changed her mind about him? An assassin had instincts as sharp as a needle point. Could those instincts have alerted Prudence Johnson to his mission? Was her unexpected advocacy in his favour a ruse to get him to drop his guard? It would be reasonable for the asssassin to assume that there could be a governor's agent on his or *her* tail. In his experience as a Confederate secret agent, it had been normal to assume that his scheme was known to the enemy, and to act accordingly. Is that what Prudence Johnson was doing? Befriending him to lessen suspicions of herself? The organization she had founded was rabidly white supremacist. The governor's equality legislation would be as poison to her.

Was Prudence Johnson the friend by day who would become his enemy by night?

And what about Kate Branigan? She, too, was his advocate. He had the devil's own job imagining the delectable Kate as an asssassin. However, casting his mind back to the eve of Shilo, he recalled a woman as wholesome as an angel; an angel with a pistol under her nurse's cloak. Was his reluctance to countenance Kate in the scurrilous role of assassin more to do with his burgeoning feelings for her?

What did he know about Prudence Johnson and

Kate Branigan? Other than the scant details that had been passed through his cell window by Colonel John Stewart, who had also played a defining role in his arrest from the Bell Creek hotel veranda a short time previously. Prudence Johnson was a righteous firebrand who believed in racial purity. But would she go so far as kill for those beliefs? She had been vehemently opposed to him being on board the stage as, in her opinion, a gambler would come under the heading of *dregs*. Or had her instincts even kicked in then? Had she seen a possible adversary in him? Now she was championing his cause. Strange? Or a genuine change of heart, brought on by the Indian attack?

How much of the *Bell Creek Sentinel*'s fiery rhetoric did Kate Branigan believe in or support? It wasn't necessarily the case that if you lived in the castle, you liked the king. Was the very lovely Kate that devious?

And what of the other passengers?

Amos Stradden was a rancher with wealth beyond that provided by the range he ranched. Where had that wealth come from? Brabbin recalled the thumbnail sketch of Stradden which had been passed through his cell window. The rancher was a Kentuckian who had deserted the Confederacy to fight for the Union. A traitor or hero? Depended on what uniform you wore. Had he, like others when it became clear that the Union would be victorious, switched sides to reap the benefits of being in the right camp? Was his motivation strictly self-interest? Would he have the ranch he now had, if he had ended the war as a Reb? Had he, again like others, filled his pockets from the towns that fell to them in the final weeks of the war, and then crossed lines to see the war out on the right side and benefit from their ill-gotten gains?

He had whipped a Negro who worked for him to within an inch of his life for stealing food from his kitchen. Evidence of his hatred for Negroes, perhaps? Maybe evidence too of how repugnant the governor's equality legislation would be to him? Repugnant enough to make him want to stop the governor's plans dead in their tracks?

And what about Walter Hanley? Of him he knew nothing. A last-minute passenger who had availed himself of a seat left vacant by illness. His good fortune? Or a well-planned ploy?

That left just Sheriff Spencer and Gertrude Bletchley. Spencer, Brabbin reckoned, he could rule out. He was a lawman with a fair and just reputation in dealing with all men. And he would not be on the stage at all, if it weren't to escort him to Cheyney.

Miss Bletchley, a strong supporter for his shackling, was not the stuff of assassins surely? On the other hand, could it be that she wanted him bound for her own nefarious reasons? It did not take much to kill a man – just a second and the opportunity. And the governor, being a politician, would never scorn an old lady or a baby. They were worth a lot of votes. It would make him mighty unpopular should he shun a sweet old dear like Gertrude Bletchley. He dismissed his seeing Gertrude Bletchley in the role of assassin as fanciful.

And what about Andy Wright and Lew Crowley? Long-time Fargo employees. Both of whom could be in Cheyney without questions being asked, and above suspicion. All he knew about the two men was that they were loyal employees of Wells Fargo, and had both shown their allegiance to the Union flag.

All in all, Ace Brabbin figured that the only ones he could safely rule out as the governor's assassin were Luther Spencer and Gertrude Bletchley.

'On board,' Spencer ordered the gambler, Hanley having secured his hands to the point of cruelty.

Climbing on top, Wright joked, 'Mebbe Fargo should hire you for every trip, Mr Stradden. If you can scare off 'Paches, think of how far and how fast road agents would run.'

Wright's whip cracked.

'Yeeeehaaa!'

The stage rolled.

Ace Brabbin's gaze went in turn to each one of his fellow-travellers, looking for the chink in the assassin's mask. Which one of them was wearing it? He saw nothing. Whoever it was who wore the mask, he or she wore it to perfection. Giving no hint of the dark secret behind it.

NINE

Ron Abbot outlined the plan for apprehending the governor's would-be killer to Ace Brabbin.

'As drawn up by Colonel Stewart,' he said.

The gambler was relieved. Any plan which John Stewart had thought through would be a good and flawless one. He had been one of Stewart's secret agents in the war, and had come to appreciate the Georgian's meticulous planning and devious turn of mind.

'You'll head for a town called Bell Creek,' Abbot had outlined. 'Working your way, you understand. Plying your trade as a gambler in saloons along the way. Your arrival in Bell Creek must be the end of a natural progression,' he warned Brabbin.

From the outset, Abbot had tried to hide his disdain for Brabbin, but the diplomatic front he had fostered had crumbled. Gamblers did not rate high on Ron Abbot's social scale. He was not alone. In the West, gamblers were not the kind of folk you invited along to the house, or let your daughter dally with on the porch of a moonlit evening. Brabbin could understand folks' reservations, since many gamblers were also gunfighters dolled up in fancy duds – like an apple with rosy skin but rotten innards.

But there were also gamblers who dealt a clean deck, and who only used a gun when pushed by a fella who reckoned he'd been cheated, pride not letting him admit that he was a lousy card-player to begin with. There was also the young turk who fancied planting a gambler to enhance his reputation as a fast gun. No matter what the circumstances of the occasion, it was Ace Brabbin's experience that the gambler always came out of the skirmish dirty. He supposed it was a natural reaction when the card-player's poke had been fattened by the citizens' money.

'Time is short,' Abbot had gone on, 'but we've got to make your arrival in Bell Creek seem natural. Newcomers,' Abbot's face soured, 'particularly a gambler, always raise people's curiosity. So Colonel Stewart has arranged what you might call an itinerary of your progression to Bell Creek.'

He had slid Brabbin a route map across the governor's highly polished desk. The gambler glowered.

'It'll make it easier for the agents along the way to support you, should you need assistance.'

'Hold it right there!' Ace said. 'Agents along the way, you say?'

'Yes, to render assis—'

'You mean to watch every move I make, don't you?' the gambler grated. Uncompromisingly, he said: 'If I take this job, which I'm beginning to doubt that I will, I'll do it my way, or the hell I won't do it at all!' He had leapt out of his chair ready to leave, and had demanded of Abbot and the governor: 'What's it to be? My way or not at all, gentlemen.'

'Colonel Stewart—'

Again, Ace Brabbin's interjection was swift and even more spiky. 'Did not draw up a plan to have me watched,' he said confidently.

At that juncture the door to a room off the governor's office had opened to reveal John Stewart, smiling broadly. 'I told you, Abbot, that Robert Brabbin would not be molly-coddled.'

Since Brabbin had renewed his acquaintance with his former boss, the colonel had insisted on giving him his proper name of Robert, positively shunning and grimacing at the appellation of Ace.

Abbot scowled at Stewart's intervention. The governor's aide was not reticent about stating his views on the advisability of entrusting the governor's safety to a gambler 'and a Reb'.

'Reb!' Stewart's normally pale complexion suffused with anger. '*I'm* a damn Reb, Abbot,' and more respectfully, 'Governor, sir.'

The governor was swift to rebuke his aide and placate John Stewart, who had proved by his action in joining the Union secret service that he fully accepted the outcome of the war, while never denying his preference for a Confederate victory.

'Colonel, I'm sure Mr Abbot did not mean to doubt your loyalty to me and the Union,' the governor said. His gaze settled on Ace Brabbin. 'And any man whom you think fit to serve. You gentlemen will accept my apologies?'

Both men had.

'Mr Abbot,' the governor had demanded.

'I'm sorry, Colonel, if I gave offence,' the governor's aide apologized. 'But I'm sure you'll understand my concerns for the governor's well-being.'

Colonel John Stewart had stood proudly, and Ace Brabbin had taken pride in his stance.

'I share those concerns, I assure you, sir,' Stewart had replied. 'And it is because I share them, Governor, that I unreservedly recommend that Brabbin be given a free hand in rooting out this cur of an assassin.'

Unhesitatingly, the governor replied: 'So be it, Colonel.'

Abbot sniped, 'Does that mean we ditch your plan, Colonel Stewart?'

'Not at all,' had been Ace Brabbin's instant reply. 'Colonel Stewart's plan is just fine.' His gaze had settled on Ron Abbot. 'Without the mollycoddlers you thought necessary, Abbot.'

Bowing out ungracefully, Abbot suggested to the governor: 'Then perhaps the responsibility for this whole operation should rightly pass to Colonel Stewart, sir.'

The governor had not contradicted his aide's view.

And so it was that over the next three weeks Brabbin had made his way steadily towards Bell Creek, making his arrival just another stop on the trail.

'Don't figure that rear wheel will make it over that hill track to Indian Creek,' Andy Wright opined, having brought the Concord to a halt as the stage's progress became more erratic, being dragged to one side by the wheel that had been damaged when it had ridden a boulder earlier on. 'That track, as I recall, offered perilous passage at the best of times. Now, without even prospectors' mules trekking it, I reckon it'll be shot to pieces.'

He stepped back to examine the wobbling wheel.

'I reckon the rigours of that hill trail will put paid to that wheel in no time at all.'

'What do you suggest, Andy?' Sheriff Spencer asked.

'You folk to spend the night at Banyon, I guess. While I go on ahead to Indian Creek relay station, rustle up a spare coach and bring it back here. Unladen, this old gal,' he patted the side of the

Concord like a loving father might the apple of his eye, 'might just about make it to Indian Creek.'

'Stay out here with Indians on the prowl?' Prudence Johnson protested.

Gertrude Bletchley asked Wright: 'Have you forgotten, sir, that my niece is waiting for me in Cheyney?'

The Fargo driver sighed. 'No ma'am, I ain't forgotten. But, like I said, this stage has had its final run with you folks on board.'

Prudence Johnson continued her protest about being abandoned with Apaches on the prowl.

Kate Branigan said: 'We've got Mr Stradden.'

'What's that suppose to mean?' Prudence Johnson questioned the reporter.

'Well,' Kate explained, 'Mr Stradden seems to have the hex on the Apache. All he has to do is wave at them and they take off.'

Kate Branigan's words struck a chord with Brabbin. What she had said was true. But why was it true? The gambler let his mind drift back to when Amos Stradden had climbed on to the roof of the stage. Back then he had thought that the rancher's bravery was admirable. But what if . . .?

Out of the blue, a flaming arrow thudded into the stagecoach door and scattered Brabbin's thoughts. But it was only a warning; the Apaches letting them know that they were still watching them. Everyone's eyes scanned their surroundings, but Brabbin knew that they were wasting their time. If the Apache did not want to be seen, then they would not be seen. Considering that the flight of an arrow in the stiffish breeze that had blown up would be precarious, and that yet it stood quivering dead centre of the stagecoach door, meant that the Indians were almost within touching distance. Yet there was little in the way of cover in the flat, featureless terrain.

The arrow had a startling effect on the group. Prudence Johnson became hysterical, needing Kate Branigan's comforting to console her. Walter Hanley, though not as strikingly upset as Prudence Johnson, was, none the less, shaken.

Luther Spencer, a tough-as-cowhide old-timer, had experienced all that the country had to throw at a body, but was still taken aback by the arrogant Apache reminder. Andy Wright and Lew Crowley were old hands at skirmishes with the Indians. However, this time, with a crippled stage and a team on its last legs, and faced with the choice of spending a night in a ghost town or risking a trail that could throw up a thousand surprises, any of which could be their undoing, their options had in the past been better.

Brabbin saw in Amos Stradden's eyes a new apprehension to replace the cockiness which he had exuded since his appearance on the stage roof had sent the Apaches scurrying. Thinking back on that extraordinary event, Brabbin found it all the more mystifying. In fact it made no sense at all.

Had the Indians decided to call off the attack anyway, and Stradden's appearance simply coincided with that decision? True, the rancher was an impressive cut of a man. But to throw a scare into the Apaches?

And for the first time too, the gambler had seen a hint of fear in Kate Branigan's emerald-green eyes. All of them would know how the Apaches liked to taunt their victims. And the fact was that they were at the Indians' mercy. Should they attack again, there could hardly be any doubt about the outcome.

'We should take our chances and head for Indian Creek,' Stradden announced.

'Mr Stradden is right,' Miss Bletchley said.

Gertrude Bletchley showed no sign of the fear a white woman should, when on the receiving end of Apache attention. Maybe, Brabbin figured, she considered herself too old for even an Apache to be interested in. If that was her assumption, she was dangerously deluded.

'What's it to be Sheriff?' Andy Wright asked, looking to the lawman for a decision. 'Do we risk heading straight for Indian Creek over that hill trail? Or hold over in Banyon?'

Clearly, Spencer did not relish having to make the decision.

'Banyon's got cover of a kind,' Ace Brabbin put into the gap that Spencer's indecision was leaving. He pointed to the stormheads racing in from the south, their blackness split by ragged lightning. 'Darkness will come soon. And if that storm heads our way it's going to dump a whole lot of rain on us and that hill trail.'

Luther Spencer said: 'Brabbin's making a lot of sense, I reckon.'

Ace Brabbin was beginning to figure, that with him having so little success in unmasking the governor's assassin, it might be a good idea to delay as long as possible. Arriving late in Cheyney could mean that the governor would have come and gone.

'We must press on,' Gertrude Bletchley insisted.

'Better late than not at all, ma'am,' Spencer growled. 'We'll stop-over at Banyon.'

Amos Stradden again ardently supported Gertrude Bletchley's demand that they press on. But Spencer stood firm.

'Banyon it is,' Andy Wright declared. 'It would be real helpful if you folks could crowd one corner. Take the weight off that busted wheel some.'

The Fargo driver cracked his whip.

Prudence Johnson said fearfully: 'I hear that Indians don't fight at night.'

'Don't,' Wright said. 'But it ain't night. And won't be for a goodly spell yet.'

'It'll be a long night,' Kate Branigan said.

No one disagreed.

'We're almost out of ammo,' said Spencer

No one disagreed.
'We're in deep trouble,' Lew Crowley said.
Again, no one disagreed.

TEN

By the time they reached Banyon, limping along as they were, daylight was fading fast. It looked like the storm would not come their way, but its presence had darkened the sky to premature night. The stage was now lurching precariously to one side, and it looked like the rear wheel was about to split open. Several more cracks had appeared in its spokes and rim, which left no doubt at all that they would not be riding the creaking Concord over the hill trail to Indian Creek.

The former mining town, born out of the promise of a fist-sized nugget found in the black-faced mountains overlooking the site, had died as quickly as it had sprawled, many of the decaying clapboard buildings still unfinished when the promised riches in the mountains fizzled out. The Banyon Nugget as it was called, after the grisly old man who had panned it in a high mountain

79

stream had vanished too, in the hands of the unknown thieves who had bushwhacked Sprinty Banyon five minutes after he had foolishly declared his discovery to those whom he'd thought were friends, who, like him, had spent a lifetime searching for colour.

'Spooky old place,' Kate Branigan said, looking into the deep, purple shadows that would soon have their secrets and ghosts shrouded in darkness. 'I feel like there's a thousand eyes watching me right now.'

Walter Hanley laughed shakily. 'Hope they're not Apache eyes.'

Kate romantically opined: 'No, Mr Hanley. These are kind eyes I feel on me. A little curious too, maybe.'

'Probably trying to figure out why in tarnation anyone would want to come to this stinking hole!' Amos Stradden grumbled.

'What if the Indians creep in here during the night?' Prudence Johnson fretted, her hand going to clutch at the collar of her blouse to pull it tighter.

'I reckon we could be in more danger from four-legged predators,' Ace Brabin said. 'We better keep fires going to warn off any cats or any other critter lurking.'

Banyon was a dour, depressing place. What little light there was under the shadow of the mountain, was quenched by the timbered slopes on opposite sides of the valley. The sighing wind added to the sense of isolation. Creeping in and out of the higgledy-piggledy buildings, it gave the feeling of ghosts whispering. Outside what was once Yang's laundry, a wind-chime stirred by the breeze tinkled lonesome music.

The wind-chimes took Brabbin's mind back to Prosperous, the Alabama plantation he had managed before the war. On its veranda there was a string of wind-chimes, constantly interchanging their haunting music in the soft breezes that sprang up in the balmy nights.

Emily Prosperous, with the honeyed skin inherited from her English grandmother, was a sight who had left Robert Brabbin breathless on encountering her in his first day of service when he had called to the house to give an account of his stewardship to Wellington Prosperous, proudly named after the famous Duke.

Prosperous had invited him to stay, shrewdly catching the way his daughter had looked at him, and he at her. Suitable men were in short supply in Alabama, most looking to pick up an easy life and fortune through marriage. Brabbin was soon to learn that Wellington Prosperous had seen more than one of them off his property at the end of a shotgun. Brabbin had no fortune, but he was soon to learn that in him Prosperous had seen a possible suitor for Emily.

'You work hard and you work honestly,' he had

told Brabbin, a year into his time at Prosperous. 'And you have managed Prosperous shrewdly and well.'

Brabbin had basked in glory. Compliments from Wellington Prosperous were as rare as snowflakes in summer.

'Why don't you call to the house for dinner this Sunday,' Prosperous had invited.

At that gathering of distinguished guests talk was of war with the North. Some were all for it. Others were less enthusiastic, even fearful, seeing a country fraught with hatred and recrimination irrespective of who the victor was.

'Best to get the thing settled,' one elderly gentleman had said. 'Foolish talk of freedom is unsettling my slaves.'

Brabbin and Emily had, as soon as was decent, gone into the flower-fragrant garden. They had spoken little before they kissed, and after had not spoken at all. There was no need for words.

The war had come. He had donned grey. Prosperous had been burned. Emily too had perished, trying to rescue her father who had been laid low with fever.

Word of Emily Prosperous's death had reached him as he passed silently through Union lines on a spying mission. It was that particular venture into Union-held territory, and the subsequent demolition of a munitions dump, which had earned him the Union appellation: Grey Ghost.

The news of Emily's death had made it a
hollow, bleak triumph. There had not been a
woman in Brabbin's life since – not as a woman
should be. There had, of course, been fleeting rela-
tionships, and hurried, mostly unsatisfactory and
unfulfilling gropings in cathouses and saloons.
But never another Emily Prosperous.

'Who was she, Ace?'

Brabbin looked to Kate Branigan, who had
come to stand alongside him. Brabbin smiled.

'She?'

'A man only gets that kind of look when there's
a woman on his mind, and only then when that
woman means more than life itself to him.'

'You're a shrewd woman, Kate,' he said. 'How
did you learn to sift a man's thoughts like that?'

'I guess by doing the same thing as you're
doing, Ace,' she answered quietly. 'Thinking about
a man who meant the world to me. The man I was
going to marry.'

There was nothing to say. The silence dragged
on for a spell, before Brabbin asked:

'Dead?'

'Dead,' she confirmed. Then, bitterly:
'Murdered.'

'Sorry.'

She said: "Shot down under a flag of truce.'

'He was a soldier?'

'Yes.'

'Union?'

83

'Confederate.'

'Flag of truce, you say?' the gambler questioned.

She nodded.

'Jeb Cross found himself and a small group of men trapped. Last days of the war. He saw no use in sacrificing his men to superior forces, so he surrendered. Got shown as much mercy as a rabid dog.'

'Tough break,' Brabbin said. 'But it happened on both sides. That's the thing about war, Kate. Its poison makes men do awful deeds.'

Her laugh was harsh and grating.

'The thing about war, too, seems to be that good men die. Killers get to be governor.'

The hair on the back of Ace Brabbin's neck stood up.

'Governor?' he said neutrally.

'Yes. Our beloved and now so upright governor was, I believe, the officer in charge of the Union forces that day.'

The shock curled in Brabbin's stomach. Cold fingers tripped along his spine. Kate Branigan had just handed him a powerful motive for assassination. He carefully measured his next question.

'So, I guess you've no cause to like our governor much, Kate?'

'Hate his guts,' she stated waspishly. 'A man like that doesn't deserve the gift of life!'

Damn! Not now, Brabbin swore silently, as

Andy Wright began organizing the night ahead, handing out various tasks.

'Why not try the hotel?' Prudence Johnson suggested, as options for sleeping arrangements were discussed.

'The hotel?' Stradden questioned stridently. His stridency was so marked that it brought all conversation to a stop.

'Looks in reasonable condition,' Walter Hanley said.

Night was creeping steadily in over Banyon. The temperature was already dropping like a stone through water.

'Not a good idea,' Brabbin said. 'Snakes. Other critters.'

'You mean we have to stay out here in the open?' Prudence Johnson asked, nervous eyes darting about her.

'Safest place,' Brabbin said. 'That way you can see what's coming at you, before it's biting your rear end.'

'The coach should be comfortable enough,' Kate Branigan suggested. 'For us ladies, that is.'

'I think I'd prefer to remain out here.' All eyes went Gertrude Bletchley's way. The old lady smiled sweetly. 'Fact is, I find the confines of the stage a little overpowering.'

'Won't you be cold?' Kate asked.

'Oh, I'll be fine by the fire, dear.'

As the arrangements for the coming night were

being discussed, Ace Brabbin's thoughts were of Kate Branigan – the only woman who had stirred the kind of feelings in him which Emily Prosperous had that first evening he had seen her on the veranda at Prosperous. Thoughts which at first were pleasing and exciting quickly turned to doubt and no small measure of trepidation, at the very real possibility of Kate Branigan being the governor's assassin. Her hatred for the man was raw and throbbing. There was no doubt about her motivation for wanting him dead. Revenge was one of the most potent forces there was. Kate Branigan, he decided, for all the wrong reasons, would need careful watching.

'How long will it take us to get to Cheyney, driver?' Miss Bletchley enquired of Andy Wright, in her tiny, china-delicate voice.

'Can't say, ma'am. Annie, that's that old rattle-box of a stage, is all tuckered out.' Wright's eyes became dreamily sad. 'The old gal would fall apart on the rigours of the hill track, I reckon.'

'Annie?' Kate Branigan queried.

The Fargo driver's gaze was full of memories whose glow told them that they were happy ones. He explained. 'Named the Concord after my late wife, rest her soul.' He chuckled. 'Now some folk think it strange, even downright insultin' and disrespectful to name a stage after Annie. But I reckoned it was what she'd want. She rode that old Concord with me many a time, and gave road agents and any other critters bent on mayhem short shift at the end of a shotgun.'

He looked with loving remembrance at the sagging stage.

'And I reckon she still rides that old rattle-trap with me each trip.'

The imagery which Wright's words conjured up stilled everyone's tongues, except Gertrude Bletchley's, who again reminded the driver about her need to get to Cheyney where her niece would be fretting about her.

'Come sun-up,' Wright promised the old lady, 'I'll make tracks for Indian Creek. Get a coach or a wheel back here for Annie. Mebbe get some on-going traveller to carry word of our plight to Cheyney to your niece, ma'am.'

Though it was the best scheme on offer, Andy Wright's plan did not find favour with the old woman. She again stressed her urgent need to reach Cheyney. Conscious of eyes on her, she explained:

'Emma, my niece, has lung problems. Picked up an infection at a clinic she worked in. The one in the mountains to the south of Cheyney, run by that German doctor who specializes in lung diseases. Worry causes her great distress.'

'Heard of that place,' Stradden said. 'I hear that fella is making mighty strides with this wasting disease they call consumption.'

'Oh, yes indeed. My Emma says that Dr Hauser

is a gifted physician.'

'Well, I don't know what I can do, ma'am,' Wright said. 'Other than what I've already said I'd do.'

As she addressed the driver, Gertrude Bletchley's bright button eyes pleaded with her fellow-travellers.

'Correct me if I'm wrong, sir. But I expect that the strain of carrying *all* of us is the greatest problem?'

'That's so, ma'am,' Wright confirmed. 'Don't help that busted wheel none.'

Gertrude Bletchley's plea to her fellow passengers intensified.

'But if I was the only passenger?'

Wright said: 'It would help, sure enough.'

'I suppose you good folk think me terrible for suggesting such a thing,' Miss Bletchley fretted. 'But under the circumstances, I do hope you'll understand and kindly indulge me.'

Their were no objectors.

'It's settled then,' the old lady said, greatly relieved. 'Emma and I will keep you good people in our prayers always.'

Wright was worried.

'Thing is, Miss Bletchley, ma'am. That wheel might still give way. That would leave us stranded, with Indians on the prowl. I don't know if I could take on that responsibility.'

'I'll take my chances for my Emma,' Gertrude

Bletchley said sternly. 'God willing we'll make it, Mr Wright.'

It was settled.

ELEVEN

At the meeting with the governor, Colonel John Stewart outlined his plan to get Brabbin on board the stage to Cheyney.

'A couple of days before you arrive in Bell Creek, I'll arrange to have a dodger dropped on the sheriff's desk. He'll be familiar with your face when you put in an appearance. A day or so later, I'll have the Wanted poster followed by a wire, requesting your apprehension should you arrive in Bell Creek, and your delivery to a US marshal at Cheyney by the next stage, which will be the one with the assassin on board, of course.'

'What if the sheriff shoots me on sight, Colonel?'

'Luther Spencer isn't that kind of man, or lawman. He'll do things by the book.'

Brabbin smiled. 'I sure hope you've got that right, Colonel.'

John Stewart did not appreciate the gambler's wry humour. He was not a man given to humour, seeing life as a journey to be completed, straight and upright. Frivolity was not in his nature. He went on:

'Of course, you'll play your part and challenge the sheriff.'

'Risky, Colonel,' Brabbin opined. 'As a gambler I've had to learn the ways of a gun. What if I beat the sheriff to the draw? And what if I don't?'

'Sheriff Spencer is a careful man. He always has his deputy in the wings. Which will allow you to save face, and make your arrest believable. Everything about this operation has got to be just that – believable. I'll arrive in town on a pretence of business a couple of days before you. I'll book in at the hotel which is right across the street from the Cat's Tail saloon, where you'll head for on your arrival in town. I'll be on hand to help out should anything go awry.

'Some problem?' Stewart had asked, as Brabbin became thoughtful.

'Well, Colonel, I can't help but wondering why you'd want me? I reckon you'd have a lot of good men whose services you could call on.' Brabbin's smile was a wry one. 'It wouldn't be that you want me out of saloons and into a respectable life again. Now would it, Colonel?'

Brabbin was well aware of John Stewart's strong Baptist beliefs. He was a man who lived a rigid and straight life, shunning the pleasures that most men sought out. The life of a saloon gambler would not meet with his strait-laced approval.

'If redemption from your present, less than salubrious life comes as a benefit of this assignment, Robert,' he stated bluntly, 'then I'll not quibble with that.'

Brabbin grinned. 'Figured you might not, Colonel.'

'Best get a fire going,' Andy Wright said. 'Night's closin' in fast.'

'Ain't much 'round to burn in the way of fuel,' Amos Stradden said.

The exchanges between the Fargo driver and the rancher shook Ace Brabbin free of his mental ramblings.

'Ain't that a fact,' the driver said, glancing about the semi-desert terrain.

'There'll probably be old furniture in the hotel we can break up and burn,' Brabbin suggested.

'Nothing there. The hotel's cleaned out.'

Brabbin wondered how Amos Stradden could know that.

'Been in Banyon recently?' he asked the rancher.

'First and last visit,' he laughed. He waved his hand about. 'Nothing to visit for, is there?'

Brabbin quizzed: 'So how come you knew the

hill trail to Indian Creek was not in the best condition, and now you can tell us that the hotel is cleaned out?' The gambler's eyes would not let Stradden's escape. 'Seems to me you know a hell of a lot about a town you're visiting for the first time, Stradden.'

Stradden looked flustered, Luther Spencer stepped in.

'Stands to reason, Brabbin. Banyon's been deserted for years. Rot has set in everywhere, including the hotel. And with no prospecting in the hills, the trail is bound to have fallen into disrepair.'

'Makes sense, I guess,' Brabbin conceded. It was a good answer. He was left wondering why Spencer had been so quick to save the rancher's blushes.

Kate Branigan hugged herself. 'Didn't realize it could get this cold so quickly.'

'You ladies avail yourselves of the protection of the stage,' the sheriff said. 'We'll get a fire going – try and rustle up some grub.'

'Ain't much,' Wright said. 'Just Fargo emergency provisions.'

'We'll make do,' Spencer declared authoritatively. Then, addressing Stradden and Hanley, 'You men gather what you can to get a fire going.' He locked eyes with Brabbin. 'You stay right where I can see you every second.'

So instructed, the gambler sat with his back to

a big boulder in full view of the sheriff. Kate Branigan wandered over. They sat in silence for a spell, neither one knowing how to start a conversation. Kate eventually did.

'Kansas, I'd say,' she said.

'Smart lady.'

'My pa came from Wichita. Spoke just like you.'

'Fought in the war?' Brabbin asked.

She shook her head. 'Quaker. Didn't hold with blood-letting as a solution to problems.'

'Not a very popular belief during the war.'

Her gaze became wistful. 'Got him shot in the back.'

The conversation died for another spell, before Brabbin asked, 'Why're you headed to Cheyney, Kate?'

'To report on the governor's speech for the *Bell Creek Sentinel.*'

'A long way to come to report a dull old speech, isn't it?'

Kate Branigan glanced about her, and confided in a hushed tone, 'It's not going to be just any old speech, Ace.'

The hairs on the back of his neck prickled.

'The governor is going to announce sweeping changes to give full equality of treatment to Negroes and Indians with us white folk.'

'Is that a fact?' Brabbin said neutrally, his mind racing.

The content of the governor's speech was

supposed to be top secret, and known only to a few. Yet, Kate Branigan knew. How?

Marking time, the gambler said: 'Should make him a popular fella, don't you think, Kate?'

'Popular? Are you crazy. A lot of men died in the war. The ranchers have been forced to hire Negroes, Indians and Mexicans. It isn't any secret that the cattle barons pay little and treat badly. Equality is the last thing they'll want. Besides, most folk think what the governor plans just isn't right.'

'And you, Kate. What do you think?'

After a thoughtful lull she said: 'Oh, I don't know what to think, Ace.' Her face hardened. 'But if the governor thinks it's a good idea, I reckon I think it's a bad one!'

'The governor told you he was going to make this speech, Kate?' Brabbin probed, hoping for an answer that would let him look Kate straight in the eye. Because the fact was, though his acquaintance with Kate Branigan was a short one, he had found himself drawn to her, almost as readily as he had been enchanted by Emily Prosperous. He had no doubt that should his acquaintance with Kate flourish to friendship and more, which he was determined that it would, if Kate was not the assassin, he would have found in Kate Branigan a woman the equal of Emily Prosperous, and the great, yawning void left inside him on Emily's death would begin to heal. Kate would not be a

replacement for Emily Prosperous. He would love
Kate, maybe in a different way, but that would
take nothing from its legitimacy. Kate was a
different woman from Emily Prosperous, but her
equal in stature.

'Heck, no,' Kate laughed, in answer to Brabbin's
question. 'I'm just acting on a reporter's instincts,
Ace, and rumour. Darn it, it could be a wasted
trip, too.'

The vice constricting Ace Brabbin's heart eased
its grip. The gambler began to breathe more
easily. But his relief lasted only seconds. Doubts
again assailed him. Had Kate seen his reaction to
the knowledge she had imparted to him? And
realizing her mistake, had she quickly attempted
to cover it up?

'Strange occupation for a woman – a reporter,'
he said.

'I guess,' she said. 'But I'm not a woman much
into having babies and making apple pie.'

'The *Bell Creek Sentinel* your first newspaper?'

'Second. The first was the *Rufus Gazette*.' Kate
laughed. 'Rufus Barrington, a dyed-in-the-wool
Reb printed it and gave it away free. In the hope
that he could persuade Southerners not to lie
down with the Union.'

She turned to lock eyes with Brabbin.

'Ever hear of the *Rufus Gazette* Ace?'

He had heard. For a time everyone had hoped
that the rebellion in print fostered by Rufus

Barrington, a Mississipian, would become a rebellion in fact. But it had not. Men were tired of war and killing, and had returned to their farms and families to try and make some sense of what had happened between men who called themselves Americans.

The *Rufus Gazette* continued for a couple of fruitless years, before Rufus Barrington, too, saw the futility of his cause. In an act of defiant desperation, he had burned down the Atlanta offices of the *Rufus Gazette*.

Brabbin said: 'The *Rufus Gazette* was a real firebrand newspaper.'

'Guess it was.'

'Did you just work for it? Or did you agree with it, Kate?' the gambler asked quietly.

She sighed. 'You know, I never could be sure, Ace.'

Brabbin chuckled with an ease that his spirit was far from feeling. 'Not the kind of publication the governor would read?'

Kate laughed along with him. 'Guess not.' Then her laughter died, and she said: 'Spoke some home truths though, did the *Rufus Gazette*.'

'Reckon?'

'Wounds take time to heal, Ace,' she said wistfully. 'Grudges take time to ease. Reb and Yankee take time to forget. White and blackman time to mix.'

'So, you think that if you're second-guessing the

97

governor's intentions correctly, his policy of immediate integration is wrong?'

Kate did not speak for a long time. When she did, Brabbin's fears hiked and his spirits slumped.

'Downright foolish, I'd say.' She stood up. 'I think I'll move a little closer to the fire, Ace.'

Brabbin watched Kate, the firelight dancing in her face. And he knew that the last person he wanted to be the governor's assassin was Kate Branigan.

TWELVE

As the night wore on, the lurking Apaches gave constant reminders of their presence in the animal and bird calls by means of which they communicated. A couple of times they sent flaming arrows over the camp as a stark warning of the threat they posed. One arrow thudded into the Concord and started a fire that rapidly took hold, fanned by the curling wind that had blown up. They had quenched the fire with only the loss of the stage's right-side door, but it warned the ladies sheltering inside of the danger and disaster that might have befallen them if it hadn't been for Ace Brabbin's alertness, when the other men had dozed off. After that the ladies bedded down by the fire as best they could.

A mountain cat prowled close to the camp, causing nerves to flutter. They were swift moving and cunning creatures who had to be watched every second. Brabbin had once seen a man who had wandered off a couple of yards beyond the range of a camp-fire to relieve himself fall prey to a cat. Though Brabbin had got to the stricken man on lightning legs, he had still been too late. What was left of the man's entrails hung dangling from his innards. Brabbin had shot the man to take him out of his misery.

As the night faded and dawn approached, Brabbin dozed. Spencer had refused to undo his shackles, even after Kate Branigan had pointed out the awful danger to him in a night alive with menace.

'Can't have him unbound,' the sheriff had stubbornly said. 'We've got enough threats without adding to them.'

When Kate had continued to protest the Bell Creek lawman had answered testily:

'Ma'am, the gambler got himself into the fix he's in. If there's a price to pay, then I figure it's got to be met by him.'

Brabbin understood the lawman's caution. If their positions were reversed, he might have been as obstinate. Seeing it from the sheriff's point of view, Brabbin was a dangerous killer – the kind of man who would not hesitate to cut another man's throat, if it were to his advantage. And what greater motive could he have for doing so, than with a hangman's noose awaiting him?

'Are you really the killer the sheriff says you

are, Ace?' Kate Branigan had asked before turning in.

Brabbin had longed to take her into his confidence and his arms, and tell her that he was part of a plot to trap the governor's assassin. But how could he? Kate might be that assassin.

'I guess,' he had replied.

It had pained him to see the disappointment and hurt in Kate's dazzling, emerald eyes, and he had almost melted and told her the truth.

Sadly, she had said before departing: 'I suppose Sheriff Spencer has a point then.'

Stirring from his edgy slumber, Brabbin found that the murky grey had strings of brighter light laced through it. The night wind had become a benevolent breeze that forecast the heat of the day ahead. The gambler shifted to relieve the pressure on his right shoulder, which had taken the brunt of his weight against the lumpy boulder. He saw a quick, but silently moving, shadow within the shadows. Not an Indian. Brabbin quickly checked the faces around him.

Amos Stradden's was missing.

THIRTEEN

Quietly, Ace Brabbin slipped into the shadows to follow the fleet-footed eloper. Being hand-bound, his effectiveness in any situation which might present itself would be pretty limited. All he could realistically do was observe what the rancher was up to. It did not surprise him any that Stradden was heading straight for the decrepit hulk of what was once, according to the rotting sign, the Diamond Palace Hotel – his interest in those premises had been keen earlier, when Prudence Johnson had suggested that they should use it as sleeping-quarters.

Brabbin, door-dodging, stepped on a loose boardwalk slat that clattered. He dived into the doorway of what used to be Banyon's hardware store just in the nick of time. Stradden turned and stared along Main. He took a long time looking, ears cocked, before he continued his journey to the Diamond Palace.

Cautiously, the gambler inched out of the hardware store door, conscious now that any second the rancher might again turn to check his back-trail. When he had dived into the hardware store door, Brabbin had almost toppled helplessly over, lacking the balance that unfettered hands would have given him. He had to be mighty careful that if another emergency came up, he'd have time to seek hiding in a more measured way.

His need for caution slowed him, and considerably opened up the gap between him and Stradden. By the time he reached the crumbling edifice that had been Banyon's premier hotel during its time of high promise, the rancher had vanished deep into its murky interior. Brabbin eased through the askew door, monitoring each step to avoid stepping on anything, such as broken glass. Should that happen, it was unlikely that Stradden would again discount it as some quirk of sound, as he had the clatter of the loose boardwalk slat. He was unarmed and bound – an interloper at a mighty disadvantage. All Ace Brabbin had going for him were his wits, and sharp as they might be, they were no match for solid lead in a direct confrontation. His only weapon was stealth.

He listened. The decaying structure creaked and groaned. What he had to do in the seconds available to him, was learn to distinguish between what were the natural movements of the building, and the sounds which would herald danger.

He crossed the foyer, uncertain as to which direction to take. He had a choice of several. Which way had Stradden gone?

A door-hinge creaked. But where? The shifting edifice distorted sound, and the creaking hinge could be anywhere – close by or some distance off. Suddenly, a match flared, and its flash of light was enhanced greatly by the hotel's dense, dark interior. Its glow almost caught Brabbin flat-footed, and he held his breath as he stepped back into the gloom beyond the match's range. Had Stradden seen him? Sudden movement always caught the eye. The gambler stood stock still, every muscle tense, as Stradden held up the match above his head to extend the range of its light.

'Someone there?' he croaked.

Brabbin could see the glinting flash of the rancher's eyes as they searched the darkness.

'Is that you, Blood Wing?'

Ace Brabbin's heart stilled. Blood Wing! It sounded like Stradden knew that particular scalp-taker personally. How? The gambler's mind drifted back to the rancher's antics on top of the stage. He now understood their purpose. It was not an act of bravery, or insanity. Stradden had purposely alerted the renegade Indian to his

presence on board the stage. Of that Brabbin was
now certain. And Stradden was an important
enough personage for Blood Wing to call off his
attack.

Why?

Stradden was standing at an open cellar door.
What business could he have in the cellar of the
ramshackle hotel? He was still suspicious and
alert. However, Brabbin reckoned that if he stood
stock still, he would go undetected. If Stradden
had rumbled him, lead would be spitting his way
by now.

Then the gambler observed a new emergency –
a double emergency! A rattler was uncoiling itself
inches from his boot and very vulnerable leg, and
a shaft of early light was creeping through a crack
in the hotel wall, relentlessly slanting towards
him. It would only take seconds for the revealing
light to reach him. When it did, Amos Stradden
could not help but see him. The rattler's glistening, beady eyes were on him. The reptile's brain
was trying to gauge the threat to it. In seconds the
wily snake's instincts would kick in. Seconds
ticked. The rattler watched. The shaft of light ate
up the space towards Ace Brabbin. His heart
thundered. Sweat coated his back – cold and
sticky.

Stradden, still not certain if he was alone,
continued to peer directly at him. At least that
was how it seemed to Brabbin. Grimly, the

gambler thought that he might be playing his last hand. Was it a losing hand? Maybe even a final hand?

FOURTEEN

'Damn!'

Sheriff Luther Spencer came alert with a bang. Ace Brabbin was missing. Why the hell had he dozed? The gambler had gone on the lam, but he could also have slit every throat before he lit out. Maybe it was to his credit that he had not, but that was poor consolation to the lawman. He had lost a prisoner. In Luther Spencer's book that was an unforgivable lapse for a lawman.

His sudden activity had the others stirring. Andy Wright knew instantly the reason for the sheriff's foul-tempered outburst. Because before he had nodded off, Brabbin had been close by and was now gone.

'Told you so, didn't I, Sheriff?' Walter Hanley crowed.

Kate Branigan was quick to defend Brabbin, though why she should she was not quite sure. Having killed a man in cold blood, as he had freely admitted, the gambler should not have an ounce of her sympathy. Yet, he not only had her sympathy, but she also found herself consumed with concern for his safety.

'There's no reason to think that he's gone,' she said. 'And if he is, Sheriff, it looks like he's not the demon-killer you think he is. We're all still breathing.'

'Why wouldn't we be?' Hanley scoffed. 'Brabbin was bound, remember? He couldn't have slit our throats if he'd wanted to.'

Walter Hanley's dry reasoning brought Kate Branigan and Luther Spencer up short. While the sheriff fully accepted Hanley's reasoning, Kate frantically searched for a counter argument. She found none. That came from the genteel and quiet-spoken Gertrude Bletchley.

'It doesn't make sense to me that Mr Brabbin should abscond in such a climate of danger, bound as he was.' All eyes were on the calm old woman. 'He would be pretty helpless if he faced a threat to his well-being. He was a whole lot safer staying right where he was.'

Kate Branigan kissed Gertrude Bletchley on the cheek. She was puzzled.

'I guess you've got a point at that, Miss Bletchley,' the lawman grudgingly agreed.

'Why, thank you Sheriff Spencer,' she said in her china-delicate voice. 'Though we shouldn't discount the wily nature of the man. Maybe he managed to wear his rawhide shackles off on that boulder he took to sitting against?'

'If he did,' Kate chanted triumphantly. 'He still didn't slit our throats.'

It was a point well scored, and intensely pleasurable to boot. Kate again thoughtfully considered the diminutive and soft-spoken Gertrude Bletchley, and her puzzlement was even more acute.

Andy Wright examined the boulder for fragments of Brabbin's rawhide bond, running his hands over it. 'No sharp or jagged edges,' he declared, and added, 'Too smooth to cut through Babbin's rawhide bracelet.'

Prudence Johnson said: 'On foot, too. The stage team are all present.'

Walter Hanley said disgustedly: 'Looks like Brabbin's captured your hearts, ladies.'

'Well, now,' Miss Bletchley smiled, 'Mr Brabbin cuts an imposing figure for a woman's heart to ignore, sir.'

Prudence Johnson became flustered. 'Mr Brabbin doesn't affect me in that way at all, Miss Bletchley. Of that I can assure you.'

The old woman's smile was a sly one.

Kate Branigan said nothing at all, because she was much too busy pondering on Gertrude Bletchley's opinion of the suave, handsome gambler. The flutter in her own heart made her feel quite giddy.

Sheriff Spencer slumped into a thoughtful mood – baffled.

'Mr Stradden is missing too.'

Prudence Johnson's announcement added new urgency to the situation.

'Prob'ly gone after Brabbin,' Lew Crowley speculated.

Slowly, ever so slowly, Ace Brabbin raised the toecap of his boot, inviting the rattler to slide his ugly head underneath it. Its tail reared up; its rattle striking a discordant and terrifying note – a sound which chilled a man's blood to below zero.

'Damn rattlers,' Amos Stradden swore, and passed through the cellar door.

Ace Brabbin brought his boot down on the snake's head and crushed it. He leaned back against the dank wall and breathed deeply. He'd had a close call, which thankfully he had survived. He took it as an omen of good fortune.

He hugged the hall wall, edging closer to the cellar door, alert for Stradden's sudden re-emergence from the cellar. Brabbin was acutely aware that all he could do by way of self-defence was charge at the rancher should he show, and hope to pitch him back down the cellar steps. Because he was now certain that Stradden's visit to the crumbling hotel had sinister implications. What they might be, he did not know. But Brabbin was certain that whatever the purpose of the rancher's skulking was, he would not want it known.

Shaking himself free of his bafflement, Spencer instructed: 'Andy, Mr Hanley, if you'd oblige gentlemen, I'd like you to fan out. See if you can pick up Brabbin's sign. He can't have gone that far, I reckon.'

'Maybe the Apaches got him.'

Kate Branigan glowered at Hanley's spiteful remark. 'Sounds to me as if that would please you, Hanley,' she said angrily.

'I won't deny but that it would, Miss Branigan.' His tone became scoffingly derisive and critical. 'I don't wear a petticoat, so Brabbin hasn't got the kind of fascination for me that he has for you.'

Hot colour rushed to Kate's face. His stinging riposte held more than a modicum of truth in it.

Hanley was stunned – indeed everyone was – by Prudence Johnson's action-laden rebuke of Hanley. Her hand slapped his face. Her action set Kate to wondering whether Prudence Johnson, too, had fallen in love with Ace Brabbin. Too? It struck Kate like a bolt out of the blue that she was in love with the gambler.

Luther Spencer shook his head, now totally bewildered by events. Miss Bletchley smiled, calmly amused.

Reaching the cellar door, Brabbin put his ear to it

in an attempt to locate Stradden's position inside the cellar. It was absolutely still. He turned his back to the door and tried to turn its unoiled doorknob, restricted as he was with his hands tied behind his back. He had to be extremely careful. If the doorknob should slip from his grasp, and the lock mechanism recoiled, the rancher would know there was someone about. He hadn't given any thought yet to the creaking door-hinges. It might never come to solving that problem.

The lock clicked. The click was hardly noticeable, but it was thunderous in Brabbin's ears. He was sure that the rancher had to have heard it. He waited, tense and expectant. Nothing. No sound – no movement.

He eased open the cellar door a fraction and paused, listening. He could hear creaks in the cellar which at first were a mystery, and then became the sound of nails being prised loose, he reckoned. It puzzled Brabbin that Stradden should be drawing nails. His bafflement only lasted another few seconds, before he reached a conclusion as to what Stradden was doing. He was opening a crate.

It seemed to take an age to get the door open enough for him to squeeze through, as the door had to be opened a smidgen at a time to overcome the rusted hinges. Brabbin started down the cellar steps, hugging the wall as he progressed. He tested each step on the stairs, before cautiously bringing his weight to bear. A creaking step would leave him facing a deadly dilemma.

The glow of a lamp reached up the stairs and danced ghostily on the damp walls, like a crowd of drunken men with wayward legs.

Half-way down the stairs, Brabbin risked looking over the banister. His reckoning as to what Stradden was up to was confirmed. The rancher was prising loose the cover of a crate. The gambler's heart leaped on seeing the heavy black writing on the side of the crate. It read: WINCHESTER RIFLES.

Brabbin had the answer to Stradden's healthy bank balance. Gun-running was a mighty profitable business. Some of those who'd made their fortunes in the West had banked their first nickels and dimes from the filthy trade.

Crate opened, Stradden took out one of the spanking new repeater rifles, his eyes greedy. 'This consignment should be worth a lot of gold,' he murmured. He put the rifle to his eye to look along its barrel. His grunt was one of pure satisfaction. He picked up the lamp and took it across to a corner of the cellar, where, to Brabbin's horror, the rancher stripped a tarpaulin cover from a whole pile of crates. He stood back and laughed. There were enough rifles to start a war.

Brabbin now understood the rancher's reluctance to visit Banyon. He had been fearful of his secret being revealed. Brabbin was in a quandary.

There was nothing he could do with his hands tied behind his back. He would have to withdraw – find Spencer. He edged slowly back up the stairs, and stopped dead in his tracks.

A pistol pressed on his spine.

'This is mighty careless of you, Stradden,' the pistol-packer growled.

Ace Brabbin was wide-eyed with surprise. He swung around. Luther Spencer's gun cracked his skull.

He toppled headlong down the steps, crashing heavily on to the cellar floor. The gambler lay still, feigning unconsciousness, his senses just about with him.

'Just as well I woke up and found Brabbin had gone missing,' Spencer said, his tone sharply critical.

The note of criticism turned to suspicion. 'So,' the lawman's steps sounded on the stairs, 'this is the reason you wanted to shy off coming to Banyon, huh?' He walked past Brabbin's prone form to where the crates of Winchester rifles were. In the threatening tone of a hardcase, Spencer growled sourly, 'I don't know if it's right for you to be keeping secrets like this from your partner, Stradden.'

Partner!

Stradden laughed jitterly. 'We're partner's fair and square, Luther.'

'I hope so, Amos,' Spencer's tone was laden with

menace. 'I'd sure hate to think that you were planning on cutting me out of,' his boot kicked the crate which the rancher had opened, 'this cash-rich deal.'

'You'll get your cut,' Stradden nervously reassured the sheriff.

Spencer's laughter was hollow. 'If I don't, Amos, I'll have to jail you or . . .' he sighed heavily, and said matter of factly, 'kill you.'

The crooked lawman strolled around the cellar, as a lord might over his domain.

'Killing you, I reckon, would be the kindest thing to do. 'Cause gun-running to the Apaches would bring you a mighty long and painful stretch in the pen.'

Eager to please, Stradden promised: 'You'll get every cent due, Luther.'

Expansively, the sheriff said: 'I trust you, Amos.' Then: 'Now. What'll we do with Brabbin?'

'Kill him, of course,' the rancher replied mercilessly.

'Looks like he's already dead from that fall,' Spencer said.

Brabbin felt the prod of the sheriff's toecap in his ribs.

'You know,' Stradden said, 'never could figure why a straight-arrow lawman like you threw in your lot with me. I was sure that when you happened on me and Blood Wing trading a couple of weeks ago, you'd haul me off to jail there and

115

then.' He chuckled. 'You knocked me back on my ass when you opted for a cut of the business.'

Wearily, Spencer said: 'I knocked myself back too, Stradden. Never figured I'd have any hand in gun-running. But the devil was tugging my tail that day.'

There was a long silence, in which Brabbin could sense the sheriff's unease – maybe regret, too.

Spencer said: 'You see, Lucy's got this damn tumour. She needs a high-toned sawbones if she's to have a chance of surviving. Know how much that costs, Stradden? A heck of a lot more than a sheriff can come up with, that's for sure.

'Lucy and me have been married for nigh on thirty years. We tied the knot when she was seventeen and I was a spit more. I just can't sit by and do nothing.'

When he spoke again, Spencer's voice was laden with self-loathing.

'If I had a choice, I'd never be a partner of dregs like you, Stradden.'

Piqued, the rancher scoffed: 'Need makes for strange bedfellows, Sheriff.' Then, dread filled Ace Brabbin's mind as Stradden said: 'Think I'll slit Brabbin's throat.'

Opening an eye a mite the gambler saw death in the gleaming blade in Stradden's hand.

FIFTEEN

'Anyone in here?'

Kate Branigan's lilting voice was the miracle Brabbin had prayed for.

'Hello . . .'

'Get Brabbin out of sight,' Spencer ordered urgently.

Kate's footsteps were directly above, approaching the open cellar door. Brabbin found himself being dragged by the legs. To keep up the pretence of being dead, he let his full weight sag, enjoying Stradden's grunts and groans as he hauled him under the cellar stairs.

'Someone down there?' Kate called.

'The guns,' Stradden said.

Spencer hared across the cellar to stow the open crate and draw back the tarpaulin. Displaying admirable quick-wittedness, he grabbed the lamp and held it aloft, as if he were searching the cellar – careful to keep its glow

away from the corner where the rifles were
stashed.

'You shouldn't be in here, Kate,' the sheriff
called sociably, as the reporter appeared in the
cellar door. 'It's dangerous. The whole place could
come tumbling down at any second.'

Kate looked curiously from Stradden to
Spencer.

The sheriff said: 'Amos and me were having a
look round down here for Brabbin. Amos saw him
make tracks and followed, but lost him.'

'No sign of Ace?' Kate asked anxiously.

Brabbin's heart was stirred by the concern in
Kate's voice.

' 'Fraid not,' Spencer answered.

'I reckon he's long gone,' was Stradden's opinion.

'Then I'll pray that he'll be safe,' Kate said, her
voice reflective and sad.

Ace Brabbin's heart leaped.

'Have you fallen for the gambler?' Stradden
asked in disbelief.

Of all the questions which Ace Brabbin had
wanted answered in his lifetime, this was the one
he wanted answered most of all. If it was the
answer he was hoping for, he'd find it mighty
difficult not to cut loose with the mother of all
yells. Along with resisting the jig which would
beset his legs.

Kate's hesitancy doused his hope. But when she

spoke, it was renewed aplenty.

'I guess I have, Mr Stradden.'

'But he's a killer,' the rancher said.

'You know,' Kate said, 'there's something about Ace that somehow contradicts that.'

Brabbin saw a new danger looming. The last thing he needed was for Kate's prompting to start Spencer and Stradden thinking along new lines, and speculating about him.

Spencer said dourly: 'Brabbin's a killer all right, Kate. Got the dodger and the wire to prove it.'

'Are you still dewy-eyed about him?' Stradden asked.

Kate said: 'I guess I was hoping . . . Pity. Ace Brabbin is the kind of man I could sit on the porch with.'

Brabbin had confirmation of Kate Branigan's love for him. The future was rosier than it had ever been – if she wasn't the governor's assassin. His high spirits dipped some.

'No point in hanging 'round here,' Spencer said.

Brabbin heard Stradden's and Spencer's foot-steps on the stairs. The cellar door slammed shut. He waited. After a safe spell he rolled out from under the stairs. He had to undo his hands. Trussed, he was helpless. He peered into the cellar's gloom. He could see nothing that would cut through the rawhide bond tying his hands. Then an idea struck him. He scrambled over to

119

the tarpaulin covering the stash of Winchesters. He tugged at it with his teeth. It was a slow, arduous task, which he hoped would be worth the effort.

It was.

The gambler smiled broadly on seeing the shining new nail sticking out of the frame of the crate which Stradden had prised open. He immediately set about scraping his bond on the glistening point of the nail. It would take a long time. He could only hope that the nail would not work loose. It had to remain firm if it was to be of use.

Slowly, each thread of rawhide was shredded, forming an ever-thickening spider's web of ragged strands. He felt the bond loosening, but there was a long way to go. Any second of which Spencer or Stradden might check back.

As time wore on, he had to force himself to continue his easy tweaking of the nail to make sure that it remained firm until it had chewed away enough to make it possible to break the bond. Time was running against him. Relentless in its march.

Brabbin had been in some binds in his time. But this was the daddy of all binds!

SIXTEEN

'I'll get a stage and help back here as fast as I can,' Andy Wright promised, as the decrepit Concord with Gertrude Bletchley on board rolled out of Banyon.

They had discussed the wisdom of Wright and Bletchley heading for Indian Creek on their own with Apaches prodding for trouble. The fact was, with its delicate rear wheel, the stage could not safely accommodate everyone. If the wheel shattered they would be stranded in hostile territory at the mercy of the Indians. A cavalry patrol searching for Blood Wing and his bloodthirsty band might happen along. But that would be handing their fate over to luck, which everyone agreed had not favoured them one little bit. Of course, different decisions would have been made, had they known that a short distance away in what used to be the Diamond Palace Hotel, there were several boxes of rifles and a plentiful supply of ammunition.

Walter Hanley watched anxiously as the stage began climbing the narrow hill-trail out of Banyon to Indian Creek. He, too, desperately needed to reach Cheyney, but for entirely different reasons from Gertrude Bletchley's. Hanley had quietly tried to persuade Andy Wright to include him as a second passenger, arguing that his business in Cheyney, without specifying its nature, was every bit as urgent as Miss Bletchley's. Wright had adamantly refused to consider Hanley's request, despite his offer of a substantial bribe. The Fargo man was taken aback that Hanley could offer as much as he had. Hanley didn't seem to be the kind of man who would be packing that kind of money.

'How long will it be before you get back here?' Hanley had enquired anxiously of the driver.

Wright had replied cantankerously, seeing Hanley as a coward on the lam, 'Can't really put a time on it, Hanley. All I can tell you is that it'll be as quick as I can make it.'

To Wright's utter astonishment, Hanley increased his bribe.

'You're offering me Judas coin, mister,' the Fargo driver had scowled. 'A lot of Judas coin. You must want to get to Cheyney real bad?'

Hanley had become furtive. 'Business,' he had muttered evasively.

Wright had sensibly not mentioned Hanley's treachery. It would have struck a discordant note, and would have soured relations at a time when they would need all the cohesion they could muster to face the Apache threat which hung over them. For some strange reason the Apaches had stayed their hand, and that did not make sense when there were easy scalps for the taking.

No sense at all.

Before he left, Wright assured the injured Lew Crowley that he'd turn around the second he reached Indian Creek and head back.

'You stop frettin' 'bout me, Andy,' his long-time friend said. 'You keep your eyes peeled for those 'Pache bastards, ya hear.'

Massaging his wrists to get his circulation going, Ace Brabbin watched the stage depart through a grime-laden window of an upstairs room at the Diamond Palace. He worried about the safety of the stage. Andy Wright, though a feisty fighter, would not stand a chance should the Indians attack the stage. A couple of bucks would be all that would be needed to snuff out the driver and Gertrude Bletchley. He observed the worried frown on Walter Hanley's face, who paced like a caged animal. Prudence Johnson, too, seemed on edge. But that was only natural in the circumstances she found herself in. Or could it be that, stranded, she was worried that she would not reach Cheyney in time to kill the governor? Could that also be what was agitating Walter Hanley? And what about Kate Branigan? She had a faraway look, her eyes restlessly monitoring the hostile country beyond Banyon. What was her worry? Apaches? Not being able to get to Cheyney? Or, the gambler's hope was, that her concern was for him.

'Why don't you just arrest everyone on the stage?' had been Brabbin's question to Colonel John Stewart. 'That way the assassin would not get to Cheyney in the first place.'

'If we did that it would save the governor, but,' Stewart had reasoned, 'only on this occasion. We still wouldn't know who the assassin was. We couldn't hold the stage passengers for ever. We'd only be postponing the evil day. The governor is planning several speeches. He or she could strike again.

'No,' he had concluded. 'The only sure way to counter the danger posed to the governor is to unmask the assassin. We're hoping that with you on board the stage, Robert, we can do that before he or she gets near the governor. Then we can interrogate the assassin to find out how deep this conspiracy runs. If it's organized or just wildcat.'

Brabbin took some consolation, but not much, from the fact that he could now discount Stradden and Spencer as the assassins. Their interests and worries lay elsewhere. He observed the two men in a huddle, and wished he could eavesdrop on their conversation.

'It's a loco idea!' Spencer said, dismissing out of hand Stradden's whispered suggestion.

'Do you want to risk putting your neck in a noose for gun-running to the Apaches?' the rancher growled. 'In our business, the last thing we need are witnesses.'

'I'm a lawman,' Spencer responded angrily. ''Sides we don't have to trade here in Banyon.'

Stradden snorted. 'And I ain't going to leave those shiny new rifles sitting here with Blood Wing snooping 'round. Do you think he'll hand over those sacks of gold, if he gets his hands on those guns first?

'And,' he went on cruelly, 'you're no lawman, Luther. You gave up your right to that badge and high-falutin' ideas the second you threw in with me.' He added with dark finality: 'There's no other way.'

Stradden's cold-eyed gaze settled on Walter Hanley, Prudence Johnson, Lew Crowley and Kate Branigan.

'You need have no part in their killing,' he said.

'No!' Spencer grabbed Stradden's hand as it drifted towards his gun.

'OK, Luther,' the rancher soothed. 'We're partners. We listen to each other, right?'

Spencer's relief was palpable. But Stradden had not given up on his murderous plan. In fact an even better plan had come to mind. He'd let Blood Wing do his killing for him. Folk might be curious about how Spencer and he escaped the Indians' wrath. But curiosity would not put a noose around his neck, like the evidence of gunshot wounds inflicted by him might, if a shrewd investigator came on the scene.

'I'm not your partner, Stradden,' the twisted sheriff flung back. 'This is a once-off deal. I don't want anything to do with your filthy trade beyond this.'

The rancher arrogantly strolled away.

'Where're you headed?' Spencer quizzed.

'To check on our merchandise.'

And make sure that Brabbin would not turn out to be a surprise package. This thought he kept to himself. He'd had quite enough of Spencer's leash.

Brabbin drew back behind the tattered drapes as Stradden made tracks for the hotel. He glanced behind him at the rubbish-strewn room, landing and stairs beyond, littered with debris that would make a quick and silent passage impossible if Stradden revisited the hotel cellar.

What rocks had he had inside his head. He had been in the cellar, surrounded by spanking new rifles and had not grabbed one of them, figuring that he'd have all the time in the world to return to the cellar once he'd completed his reconnoitre of the town and its environs. Now he was caught flat-footed and defenceless. He was not a mistake-making man. But he had now made one that would likely end in his demise.

He hurried to the landing to observe Stradden's arrival. As the rancher strode into the hotel, Brabbin suppressed the urge to leap from the landing on top of him. The drop was a long one, and if mistimed could end in serious injury. Or if Stradden's reactions were quick enough, he could shoot him as he dropped. Even if he were success-ful in his bid to overcome Stradden, the commo-tion would likely alert Spencer to the fact that he was alive. And it would take little persuasion to convince the others that he really was the killer he was reputed to be.

The resolution of the problem on hand had to be accomplished by stealth. He crept down the stairs, back to the wall, hugging as many shadows as he could, hoping he could reach the end of the stairs to throttle the rancher as he passed on his way to the cellar. But he was not going to the cellar. He was going behind the bar.

What was he up to?

Soon it became obvious. Stradden grabbed an empty bottle and smashed the bar mirror with it. The gun-runner picked up a section of the shat-tered mirror and rubbed it clean with his sleeve.

Then he held the shiny mirror up to a shaft of sunlight slanting in through the crumbling edifice. He smiled broadly as the mirror reflected the sunlight. He manipulated the mirror, sending flashing signals slicing through the gloom. He laughed cruelly. Brabbin knew what his plan now was. He was going to signal Blood Wing. That would mean that everyone would die – except Stradden and Spencer, of course.

That Kate Branigan would die was the uppermost thought in Ace Brabbin's mind. He would have to stop Amos Stradden, and take his chances with Luther Spencer.

SEVENTEEN

When the law office door burst open to reveal Judith Scott, Deputy Ned Belton paused in composing the report on a horse-theft which be was writing. Judith cleaned house for Benjamin Rankin a couple of times a week. Rankin, a bachelor, was one of Bell Creek's richest men.

'You've got to come fast, Ned,' Judith wailed.

The deputy came from behind the desk to console the distraught woman. 'Get your breath back, Judith. Tell me what's got you so all-fired up.'

Her face was bleak; her light–blue eyes flooded with tears. 'It's Mr Rankin, Ned . . .'

Five minutes later, in Rankin's study, the horror which had distressed Judith Scott so, did the same to the deputy sheriff. Rankin was sprawled across his desk, eyes wide open in wonder. The blood from his slit throat had congealed on the polished desktop, soaked up by the papers scattered about.

'I saw that stranger who left on today's stage to Cheyney, wispy sort of fella . . .'

'Hanley,' Belton immediately identified. 'Walter Hanley. Lost in a crowd kinda fella?'

'That's him.'

Belton now recalled having seen Hanley in a huddle with Rankin the day before in the hotel lobby.

'Saw him slinking out of here a couple of minutes before he boarded the stage,' Judith informed the deputy.

The deputy expressed doubt.

'Hanley didn't look like the kind of cruel killer it would take to do this, Judith.'

'I saw him,' she insisted. 'Sneaking out of here.' Judith stabbed a finger at the open and emptied wall safe behind Rankin. 'Hugging a package. The contents, I'd say, of Mr Rankin's safe, Ned.'

Motivated, Belton said: 'I'll get a wire off to Luther in Cheyney. Not that it'll do much good, I reckon. Hanley will probably have kept right on going. But you never know.'

He hurried off to the telegraph office.

Ace Brabbin's luck ran out. Amos Stradden spotted him in the mirror he was holding, just as he was about to pounce on him. Stunned, thinking Brabbin must be a ghost, the rancher quickly overcame his surprise. He spun around, gun in hand, cocked and ready.

'Hold it right there, Brabbin! I don't know how you're here. But you're sure as hell not going a step further.'

Stradden levelled his .45 on the gambler. Brabbin reckoned that, at last, as was the case with all gamblers, his luck had run out.

Andy Wright coaxed the tired team along the twisting, full of surprises hill-trail. He had made good progress, much better than he had hoped for. So far the damaged wheel had held together, but that could change any second. A rock or dip could smash the wheel. Up to now he had been lucky. His worry was that, with all his attention taken up with the vagaries of the trail, it left precious little time to reconnoitre the country around him – terrain that any second could erupt in mayhem. Being a Fargo driver he was used to taking risks; risk-taking came with the territory. But he had never before set out on a trail with a handful of bullets, a wrecked Concord, and an old woman.

'How are we doing, Mr Wright?'

The driver leaned over to see Gertrude Bletchley leaning out of the coach window.

'We're doin' just dandy, ma'am,' he called back, over the creaking and groaning of the stage.

'How long before we reach the relay station?'

'I reckon a hour or so should do it.'

'Do you think there'll be someone there to help me get to Cheyney?'

131

'Always someone comin' and goin',' Wright reassured her. 'Now I think you should get that head of yours back inside the coach, ma'am,' he advised.

Wright looked with trepidation at the steep climb ahead and the narrowness of the trail, partly washed away by recent heavy rains. So far the trail had been well shaded from prying eyes, but the steeply rising section up ahead had little or no cover, and at the top it had no cover at all. The stage would be visible to any watching eyes for well over fifteen minutes, he reckoned.

A heck of a long time in Apache country.

Brabbin gained a few minutes by Luther Spencer's arrival on the scene. But his presence would only add a couple of seconds to the gambler's life. Being in cahoots with Stradden, Spencer would have to go along with the rancher's plan to kill him.

'Why the hell didn't you stay in the cellar, Brabbin?' Spencer growled.

'Just as well that he didn't,' Stradden said. 'Remember, we don't want any witnesses to our little scheme, Spencer.'

The gambler sensed Spencer's unease with the situation, and stoked it. 'You've fallen a long way to be lying down with a snake like Stradden, Sheriff.'

'Don't have a choice,' Spencer answered gruffly.

132

Then, angrily: 'I've been a lawman all my life, Brabbin. What have I got to show for it, huh? I've got a couple of hundred dollars in the bank. Not enough for the stage and train fares back East.'

He strode to where Brabbin was under threat of Stradden's gun.

'You think I should continue to sport this badge, while I watch the only woman I've ever loved die?' He ripped the sheriff's badge from his shirt. 'Well I won't, mister.'

Brabbin could fully understand the lawman's anguish. It was likely that if their positions were reversed, he would do the same. But sympathy for Spencer's plight would not get him out of the bind he was in. And if he were killed, it would probably mean the death of the governor, too.

He asked Spencer: 'Do you think your wife would rest easy, if she knew that the money for the doctors and hospitals was stained with the blood of the innocent people those guns in the cellar will kill?'

Furious, Spencer lashed out, sending Brabbin sprawling at the end of a pile-driving fist. The gambler was quick to take advantage of the confusion. With Stradden momentarily unsighted, he sprinted for the cellar door. The rancher cut loose with a couple of wild shots which were no threat to the gambler.

'Damn it, Spencer. Don't let him get to those rifles,' the rancher roared.

Brabbin dived through the cellar door, crashing down the steps, every bone in his body rocked by the violent fall. He lay winded and aching at the end of the steps, but there was no time for self-pity. Any second Stradden would come bursting through the cellar door, safe in the knowledge that he was unarmed, and would remain so until he could get his hands on a loaded Winchester.

'Don't just stand there!' Stradden bellowed at Spencer.

Spencer said wearily: 'Let him be, Stradden.'

'Let him be?'

'Brabbin is right. Lucy wouldn't want money stained with the blood of innocents. It was crazy for me to get into this in the first place.'

'That a fact,' Stradden's voice was laced with menace.

A gun exploded.

A body fell.

Brabbin waited.

Stradden laughed. 'I sure hope you understand, Sheriff, that I just had to dissolve this partnership, with you going all righteous on me.'

The gambler grabbed a Winchester and tore open a box of bullets. He hurriedly slotted home a couple of rounds. Spencer's turn of conscience had handed him golden seconds. He waited, rifle at the ready for Stradden to appear. It puzzled him that he had not. The answer to his musing came when Stradden called out:

'I'm not risking my hide going down there, Brabbin. I've got friends a-coming, who'll kill you and everyone else for me.'

The rancher's taunting laughter faded, as he made his way to the boardwalk to signal to Blood Wing. Brabbin crept up the cellar stairs, but a bullet took a chunk out of the cellar door inches from his head.

'Come on, Brabbin,' Stradden laughed. 'What're you waiting for?'

Another bullet took a chunk out of the wall behind him.

Any attempt by Brabbin to break out of the cellar would make him a sitting target for the rancher. All Stradden had to do was bide his time. Blood Wing's arrival would solve his problems. It looked like his run of bad luck was holding.

EIGHTEEN

Blood Wing read Stradden's flashing message. Sending messages with a mirror had been a skill the rancher had learned as a Confederate soldier. He in turn had taught the Apache renegade. He could ride unobtrusively into the canyon country south of his ranch and flash his silent messages to the Apaches, as he had done on many occasions in pursuance of the devil's trade he was engaged in. Stradden's message promised guns and no opposition. They would trade, then he would kill everyone.

'We ride now,' Blood Wing ordered his bucks. 'To the town of spirits.'

Kate Branigan, seeing the flash of the mirror, alerted Hanley, Lew Crowley and Prudence Johnson.

'Damn and tarnation,' the weakened Crowley swore.

He had seen mirror-messages before. Though

136

he could not read the contents, he was certain of who the recipient was.

'What can it mean?' Prudence Johnson worried.

The wounded shotgun rider supplied the alarming answer. 'Someone's signalling them 'Pache savages.'

Astounded, Prudence Johnson asked: 'But who'd want to do that. And why?'

It was a mystery that was soon replaced by horror, as they watched the Apaches ride out of the hills.

As the Concord climbed the open trail, Andy Wright had a sense of watching eyes on him. Fact or imagination? If their luck held, and they made it over the top, the run to Indian Creek would be less arduous, and would give the horses a much needed breather. Sensing danger all round, the previous night had been a long and restless one for them. The exertions of the day before had not been slept off, and they had tired quickly. Wright's worried glance went to the side of the trail, and the long drop to a boulder-strewn ravine. If one of the team's legs gave out now, it could send the coach over the edge. *Maybes* and *ifs* suddenly went out the window.

A quartet of Apache renegades appeared at the top of the trail!

The saloon of the Diamond Palace reverberated to the explosion of a gun – not Stradden's. He was toppling backwards through the hotel door, clutching his chest, looking surprised. He raised his gun, but did not get a shot off. A second bullet split his skull open.

'Brabbin,' Spencer called weakly. The gambler sped to the lawman's side. His eyes were already rolling upwards. 'If you get out of here, tell Lucy that I love her dearly, won't you?'

Brabbin promised the dying lawman that he would. His eyes came to rest on the sheriff's badge, which Spencer had discarded. He picked it up, polished it until it glowed, and then pinned it to Spencer's shirt.

'I can't think of another man more deserving of this,' the gambler said.

The lawman's eyes rested on the badge and closed. His last breath went with a sad smile.

Kate Branigan, Walter Hanley, Prudence Johnson and Lew Crowley crowded the hotel door.

'It's a heck of a long story,' Ace Brabbin told them. The wild howls of the arriving Indians split the air. 'It's telling will have to keep.'

Kate came to Brabbin's arms. 'I guess this is the time to tell you that I love you, Ace.'

'I hope you still will fifty years from now, Kate.'

Kate's smile was a sad one. How could there be fifty years? There was a noose waiting for Ace Brabbin. If the Apaches did not slit his throat.

'Let's give those Apaches a damn surprise,' the gambler said.

*

Wright had quickly taken cover inside the Concord, not that it would matter any. The four Apaches had now become eight.

'Stay down ma'am,' the driver ordered Miss Bletchley.

He turned around sharply on hearing the rip of cloth, and his eyes popped. Gertrude Bletchley was ripping her clothing off, and toting a pair of sixguns. The carefully crafted hairbun was also gone, and in its place was short back and sides.

'I'll explain later, Wright.' To Andy Wright's utter amazement, Miss Bletchley had changed into a man! 'After we dispatch these bastards.' The man's guns bucked and two Apaches shot backwards off their ponies. 'Start shooting man,' he ordered, with the snap of a military man in his tone.

'I'll be damned,' the Fargo driver muttered, and blasted another Indian.

Another two fell to the man's ace shooting, which brought the remaining three up short and in full retreat. The man swung athletically on to the roof of the Concord. He cut down another of the bucks as they vanished over the top of the trail. He swung back into the stage, the oddest sight Andy Wright had ever seen, rouged and powdered, and holding smoking sixguns.

'Well, I said I'd explain,' the man said. 'My

name is Daniel Stewart. I'm a Southern soldier, sir.'

'A Reb? There ain't no Rebs any more,' Wright protested.

'That's where you are wrong, sir. Some of us still hold fast to our beliefs, and are prepared to fight for those beliefs; to oppose those who would put Niggers on the same level as a white man. That's why I have to kill the governor.'

Andy Wright paled. 'Kill the governor?'

'Yes, sir. He favours giving Niggers and Indians equality with the white man.'

Andy Wright was astounded. Realizing that he had become privy to a secret that he should not know, his astonishment turned to fear.

Daniel Stewart said: 'It is with regret that I do what I have to do now, Mr Wright.' He cocked his pistol. 'You're a good man. But then there were many good men lost in the war.' His features hardened to stone. 'Too many to allow lily-livers like our governor to whittle away what those men died for, sir.'

Stewart's gun exploded.

Led by Ace Brabbin, the remaining survivors of the Cheyney stage lined up on the hotel roof, Winchesters ready, praying that the rotten structure would not disintegrate under them. Lew Crowley, though exhausted and weak, would not be omitted. Brabbin's theory that Stradden's message to the Apaches had told them of little or no resistance, was proven in their swaggering approach to Banyon.

They had loaded as many rifles as there was time for. Prudence Johnson did not know one end of a gun from the other, but a quick course of instruction by Brabbin had imparted to her the rudiments of shooting a rifle. If she brought down an Apache it would be a miracle. Brabbin was counting on her wild shooting to give the Indians the impression that there was a small army on the hotel roof.

'Just keep pressing the trigger, Prudence,' the gambler had instructed her.

Kate Branigan was reasonably skilled at using a sixgun, and probably more skilled in using that dainty derringer she packed in her vanity case, he speculated. However, using a rifle was an entirely different matter, and he could only hope that she'd be a notch above Prudence Johnson. Hanley and Crowley would give a good account of themselves. Overall, Brabbin was hoping that Blood Wing, surprised by the ferocity of the defence of the ghost town, would abandon his attack until he had time to figure out Stradden's game in leading him into an ambush.

'Hold your fire,' Brabbin ordered. The Apaches were close, but not close enough. 'A wild shot now will alert them to trouble. Wait until they reach the verge of Main before opening up.'

'Might not that be a trifle late?' Hanley questioned nervously.

Kate expressed similar reservations.

Brabbin said: 'We have to bring down as many as we can with our first volleys to make Blood Wing change his mind. If we're lucky, there'll be ponies to ride out of here.'

The Apaches kept coming.

'Any second now,' Brabbin said.

A bedraggled Daniel Stewart, back in the role of Gertrude Bletchley, staggered out of the wooded slope opposite the Indian Creek stage relay station. The station manager and his wife hurried to assist the elderly lady, as they thought.

'Indians,' Stewart explained breathlessly.

Bob Blunt and his wife helped the exhausted old woman inside the station.

'My niece,' the fake Miss Bletchley pleaded, 'she's so ill, poor thing. I must get to Cheyney immediately.'

Blunt said: 'I guess with Indians on the prowl, we'd better make tracks too, Mary. I'll ready the buckboard right now.'

'Oh, thank you kindly, sir,' the old woman thanked him.

Mary Blunt comforted the old woman. 'Don't you worry none. We'll be on our way very soon.'

'The stage, ma'am?' Blunt enquired.

The old woman shook her head.

'All dead?' the station manager asked, greatly disturbed by the news.

'After the Indians attacked the stage, we headed for Banyon . . .'

'The ghost town?' Blunt checked.

'Yes. When the second attack came . . .' The fake Miss Bletchley dropped her eyes to the floor feigning shame. 'I hid. God forgive me.'

Mary Blunt took the old woman's hands in hers. 'You have nothing to be ashamed of . . . ah . . .'

'Bletchley. Gertrude Bletchley.'

'How did you get here, ma'am?' Blunt enquired.

'I got hold of a horse. It wasn't much of a feat on my part, he was wounded and hobbling. It's been a long time since I've ridden, but I managed to make it most of the way here before the spent animal folded under me.'

'You've been very brave, Miss Bletchley,' Mary Blunt complimented.

Daniel Stewart's smile was coy. 'Oh, dear me,' he fawned. 'You flatter me too much, I fear, my dear.'

'I'll bring round the buckboard.'

Bob Blunt left the station heavy shouldered with grief for the loss of a lifelong friend, Andy Wright. Ten minutes later they were on their way to Cheyney.

Daniel Stewart was on the last leg of his journey to kill the governor.

Ace Brabbin's gaze went to each one of his partners in turn. Which one was the assassin? Did it
matter? Maybe they would never leave Banyon?
And even if they did, it would probably be too late
by the time they reached Cheyney for the assassin to do his or her dirty work.

His thoughts were interrupted by Kate's warning. 'I think Blood Wing's smelt a rat.'

The wily renegade leader was waving to his
bucks to slow their approach to the town. Each
Apache in turn became suspicious of the town's
stillness. They were not as close as Brabbin would
have liked, but he had no choice. He could not let
the Indians fall back and regroup. Surprise was
the only thing they had going for them. He
ordered:

'Fire!'

The roof of the Diamond Palace Hotel erupted
in gunfire. Brabbin was pleased to see most of the
first string of Apaches topple from their ponies. In
the confused seconds that followed, more fell to
the spitting Winchesters. A half-dozen yelling
Indians rode helter-skelter for the hotel. Brabbin,
dragging Kate with him, quickly changed positions to try and down the Indians. If they
managed to get inside the hotel, they would have
a battle to fight within and without.

Blood Wing ordered the remainder of the renegades back out of range of the Winchesters to await the outcome of the bucks' sprint for the hotel. Brabbin and Kate raked the street with gunfire, felling two more Apaches. With the threat from the main war party in abeyance, Hanley and Prudence Johnson joined Brabbin and Kate in trying to stop the charging Indians from reaching the hotel and gaining entrance.

One of the six made it through. Brabbin hurriedly left the roof. Coming from sunlight into the uncertain light of the hotel's interior was a disadvantage that the gambler could have done without. The couple of minutes which the Indian had had inside the hotel would have adjusted his vision to the darker interior, handing him the advantage in the first vital seconds.

Ace Brabbin got only a fleeting glimpse of him before the Apache sprang from the shadows, tomahawk raised to split open the gambler's skull. Brabbin dodged the killer blow, but the Indian kicked out, catching him squarely in the midriff. His guts crimped, and his head spun. The Winchester fell from Brabbin's grasp. The Indian dived for it. The gambler, unable to match the young buck's agility, tore loose a shattered banister rung, and, as the Indian straightened up, he rammed the jagged-edged makeshift weapon into his gut. Blood erupted from the Apache's mouth. He triggered the rifle, but his shot went wild. Ace Brabbin again rammed home the improvised

145

lance, hoisting the Indian over the banisters. He crashed down into what used to be the lobby of the Diamond Palace.

Taking a few seconds to regain his wind, the gambler went downstairs, grabbed the dead Indian, dragged him to the door, and flung him out on to the street. Blood Wing, stunned by the doggedness of Banyon's defenders, did what Brabbin was hoping he'd do. He called off the attack.

Brabbin went to the centre of Main to round up the wandering Apache ponies. He called up to the roof of the defunct Diamond Palace Hotel.

'We're headed for Cheyney, partners!'

An hour later, on the steeply rising hill trail which the Cheyney stage had taken, they came across the Concord with Andy Wright's body inside.

'Damn Indians!' Walter Hanley swore.

Brabbin picked up the shreds of female attire, his thoughts deep.

'Poor Miss Bletchley,' Prudence Johnson wept.

Kate comforted the distraught woman.

The gambler was casting an eye over the scene of carnage. There were seven dead Indians. He returned to the stage and examined the Fargo driver's pistol, murmuring, 'Still three bullets left . . .' His thoughts deepened further.

'What's troubling you, Ace?' Kate Branigan asked.

'Seven dead Indians. That's what's troubling me, Kate.'

Misunderstanding the drift of Ace Brabbin's thoughts, Prudence Johnson accused fierily, 'Is that all you can think about? Dead Indians. What about Miss Bletchley and Mr Wright?'

Brabbin did not take umbrage. In the absence of his revealing his thoughts, Prudence Johnson's reaction to his apparent concern for the Apaches was perfectly understandable. He explained: 'Andy Wright's gun still has three bullets in it, but there are seven dead Indians.'

Hanley said: 'He reloaded.'

'With Apaches bearing down on him, a man wouldn't have that kind of time,' Brabbin opined. After a moment's further consideration, the gambler concluded, 'I reckon there was another shooter.'

Hanley said doubtfully: 'Miss Bletchley?'

Kate dismissed this out of hand.

The gambler leaned closer to examine Wright's chest wound. 'I'd say this is a sixgun wound. Wright was shot from close range, too. Right inside this coach, I'd say.'

Brabbin caught sight of Kate Branigan's thoughtful frown.

'Want to share your thoughts, Kate?' he invited.

She shook her head. 'It's loco, Ace. Last night when I kissed Miss Bletchley on the cheek . . .' She shook her head again. 'Makes no sense . . .'

Deadly Trail

Brabbin chuckled. 'Sense is in mighty short supply right now, Kate.'

'Well, I got the kind of feeling a gal gets when she kisses a man,' the reporter blurted out.

Walter Hanley was looking at Kate Branigan with new eyes. Prudence Johnson was on the verge of fainting.

Brabbin grinned. 'I guess you should explain that a little better, Kate.'

Angrily, Kate said: 'Not that kind of feeling. What I mean is that Miss Bletchley's face was rough. Like a man's.'

'Like a man's?' Brabbin pondered. Then, like a bolt out of the blue, the gambler understood the sense of familiarity he had experienced on seeing Gertrude Bletchley – particularly those darting, button blue eyes. He raced to his horse. 'We've got to make tracks, fast.'

Catching him up, Kate asked: 'What bug's gotten into you, Ace?'

Knowing the identity of the governor's assassin, Brabbin was relieved and overjoyed that he could at last confide in Kate Branigan. He told her the purpose of his trip, and how his arrest for murder had been orchestrated to get him on the stage to Cheyney for the purpose of unmasking the governor's assassin.

Equally overjoyed, Kate threw her arms around him, and kissed him with a passion that he was certain would make his nights – from now on –

memorable. Puzzled, she asked, 'But who is the assassin, Ace?'

'A fella by the name of Daniel Stewart – alias Gertrude Bletchley.'

Kate rubbed her cheek. 'So that's how . . . I was kissing a man!'

'That's right,' the gambler smiled. 'And from now on it's something I'm going to look on unkindly. You going around kissing every man in sight.'

'But I thought I was . . . Oh, come here, Ace Brabbin.'

She kissed him again, and his toes curled.

'You know, Kate Branigan,' he said, with a long satisfied sigh. 'You've picked the worst possible moment to perk me up like you have.'

Kate drew him even closer. 'There'll be lots of other moments, Ace,' she purred.

His grin was wide and contented. 'I'm counting on it Kate, my darling.'

NINETEEN

Cheyney was crowded with people wanting to hear the governor's speech. Already there was division in the crowd, with hecklers from opposing camps slinging insults.

Ace Brabbin made his way through the crowd keenly seeking out Daniel Stewart, or the demure Miss Bletchley, not knowing which mask Stewart would be wearing. Kate had volunteered to help, as had Prudence Johnson. Strangely, Walter Hanley had made tracks to the livery to buy a horse, stating that his business further down the trail was all important, and he did not have time to listen to the governor's speech, or indeed have any interest in his proposals for equality between all Americans.

Brabbin's intitial glee at having unmasked the assassin had quickly turned to regret, at hunting down the brother of Colonel John Stewart, a man whom he respected and admired too much to want to inflict the pain he was about to unload on him.

Brabbin was on the hotel porch scanning the crowd, when the Cheyney marshal joined him. He held a telegraph message from Ned Belton, Bell Creek's deputy sheriff.

'Where'd this fella Hanley get to, mister?' the marshal asked, his tone urgent.

'Last I saw of him he was headed to the livery to buy a horse,' Brabbin told the lawman.

The marshal's glance went in the direction of the livery, from where Walter Hanley was leaving astride a fiery-blooded stallion who would eat up fast miles.

'Sam,' the marshal hollered to his deputy, who was nearer the livery. 'That's Hanley!'

The deputy commanded: 'Hold it right there, Hanley.'

Walter Hanley, panic showing in every nerve and muscle, spurred the stallion to a gallop, scattering the crowd as he thundered out of town. The deputy carefully got the fleeing Hanley in his sights, fired once, and stopped him in his tracks.

'Wanted for murder back in Bell Creek,' the marshal explained to a baffled Ace Brabbin. 'Looks like he was guilty, too.' He called to his deputy. 'Good shooting, Sam. You've saved us the cost of conveying him back to Bell Creek for trial.'

The town undertaker was already eagerly measuring Hanley's lifeless body. However, Ace

Brabbin's interest in Walter Hanley had soon vanished. On the other side of the street, in the sudden gap which Hanley's ill-advised escape had opened up, his eyes met directly with those of a demure old woman. Both Brabbin and Daniel Stewart glanced towards the platform which the governor was climbing to deliver his speech. The crowd closed as suddenly as it had opened up, and Brabbin again lost sight of Stewart. He sprinted straight for the platform, not figuring he'd have time now to again pin-point Stewart in the crowd, which was jostling to hear the governor's address.

His only hope was to reach the governor and warn him, before Daniel Stewart got close enough to perpetrate his foul deed of murder.

'Ace!' Kate called out.

'Not now, Kate,' he called back.

'But . . .'

Kate kicked up dirt as Brabbin vanished into the crowd. She returned her glance to an upper window of the hotel, and her heart beat like a drum. The glint of sunlight on a gun-barrel was still there!

'Ladies and gentlemen,' Ron Abbot the governor's aide announced, waving his hands over the crowd for calm and quietness, 'the Governor.'

The governor strode forward to the edge of the platform, offering himself as a perfect target. Brabbin pounded up the steps, beating aside any opposition to his sprint. He flung himself at the governor, bringing him down just as a volley of shots splintered the rail of the platform on which he had just been leaning to deliver his address.

The crowd dived for cover, leaving Daniel Stewart exposed, a smoking gun in his hand, right smack in front of the platform.

Ace Brabbin leaped through the air, sixgun spitting, blasting Daniel Stewart. Shock gripped the crowd; shock that quickly turned to anger. They had never before seen a woman – an old woman at that, so brutally gunned down. Their anger was directed at Brabbin, until he revealed Daniel Stewart's masquerade and his mission. The town doctor performed a quick examination of the body to verify Brabbin's claim.

Kate Branigan drew the derringer which she carried for protection, having covered many dangerous assignments as a reporter, and eased open the hotel-room door. She was grateful for the well-oiled hinges. There was a man crouched at the room window, his rifle trained on the governor's platform at the end of the main street. He was brushing away tears, and his anger boiled.

Kate said: 'Drop it, mister.'

The man spun around to face Kate, surprise quickly changing to defiance.

'I'll shoot,' Kate warned shakily.

The man snorted, and again took up his stance at the window.

'I'm warning you,' Kate said, not sure if she would have the courage to kill the man if she had to.

The man raised the rifle. Grimly he said: 'An eye for an eye. That's fair, isn't it?'

Kate found the courage. In Ace Brabbin she had found the man she wanted to share her life with. She was not going to lose him. The derringer exploded. A red blob instantly appeared on the man's back. He stood and turned, still full of menace, and angrier than ever. Kate fired again, and this time the red blob appeared on his chest. He fell back through the window on to the hotel porch roof, and rolled off on to the street.

Ace Brabbin turned the dying man over, and was rocked back on his heels. 'Colonel Stewart, sir!'

John Stewart's smile was weak. 'I knew the governor had the right man for the job, in you, Robert.'

'The governor?'

'Yes, Robert. He wanted the Grey Ghost, the most feared Confederate agent of them all on the job.'

His sigh was weary, his eyes losing their light.

'Forgive me, Robert. Neither Daniel nor I could take defeat. I thought I could, until the governor came up with his idea that all Americans should be equal. That went against everything the South stood for, Robert.'

He gasped, his breath thin and quivering.

'Doesn't seem to matter much now.' His eyes dimmed. 'I guess in the end, nothing matters at all.'

His hands gripped Brabbin's with the last of his strength. 'Pray for me and Daniel, Robert.' His last breath left him with a quiet whimper.

Ace Brabbin stood, came to attention, and saluted.

On their way back to Bell Creek, Brabbin and Kate diverted to Banyon to take home Luther Spencer's remains for decent burial. The governor had offered a reward for his safe delivery, which Brabbin took to give to Lucy Spencer for her treatment back East. He let stand the notion of Luther Spencer losing his life in a challenge against Amos Stradden to deliver them from harm. The Bell Creek sheriff had been a good man driven to badness by his love for his wife. Ace Brabbin saw no point in muddying his name.

In a quiet moment at a camp-fire Kate said, testing the sound of Brabbin's name: 'Robert, huh?'

'That's my real name. Ace is an appellation I picked up as a gambler.'

'Speaking of gambling . . .' Kate said.

'Are you throwing a leash on me, Kate?' he quizzed.

She smiled. 'Thought about it. But I don't know

of any leash that could hold you, if you didn't want to be held, Robert.'

Brabbin joked: 'Beautiful, wise, and a handy shot, too. I'm a lucky fella.'

He did not tell her right then about his new job of protecting the governor, which one day might take them all the way to Washington, should the governor become president of the United States of America, which a whole lot of people wanted and figured he'd become one day. Before he had taken on the job, Brabbin had put directly to the governor Kate's charge that he was the officer in command the day her beau Jeb Cross had surrendered, and had told the governor quite bluntly that he'd see him in hell if the charge held up. But official records showed the governor fifty miles away from the murderous encounter of that grim day, and they also showed that the governor had duly seen that the officer in charge of the massacre had been called to book for his terrible deed.

Kate screwed up her face. 'I think I'll call you, Bob, Robert.'

'OK by me, Katie,' he said.

'Katie!' she yelped.

He cut off her yelp by taking her into his arms and kissing her – an age-old way of stopping a woman's protest.

Lying back under a yellow moon, with Kate in his arms, he said: 'You know, Katie . . .'

'Yes, Bob honey,' she answered dreamily.

'I reckon you and me are going to make a hell of a team.'

'You reckon?'

'I reckon,' Ace Brabbin said, and kissed Kate. 'Not a woman much into having babies and making apple pie, huh?'

Kate recalled her statement to that effect. She grinned. 'Well, what do you say to me skipping the apple pie, Bob?'

Ace Brabbin returned her grin.

'Fine with me, Katie. Leaves more time for making babies.'

He kissed her again. Kate Branigan gave as good as she got.